T0090463

SILENT
TWIN

Tracy Plehn

*Our mission is to efficiently provide the world's finest, most comprehensive
book publishing service, enabling every author to experience success.
To find out how to publish your book, your way, and have it available
worldwide, visit us online at www.trafford.com*

Trafford rev. 5/11/2010

 www.trafford.com

North America & international
toll-free: 1 888 232 4444 (USA & Canada)
phone: 250 383 6864 ♦ fax: 812 355 4082

Chapter One

"HELP ME!! Please, someone has to be out there! I'm down here, someone please..." Her voice was so hoarse from screaming and crying. She had no idea how long she had been held captive and didn't know if she could survive much longer. She wished that whoever these men were would just kill her and get it over with. No one would speak to her or tell her what they wanted. As far as she could tell, there were about 5 different men and one time she thought she heard a woman's voice. Twice a day some brute would bring her water and some food, if you want to call it that, it was just enough to sustain her and keep her alive, but why?

The room that held her smelled musty, it was so dark and bitterly cold. She could tell it was some sort of wine cellar but all the wine holders were empty. It had stone walls and floors and she figured it must be about a 20'x20', not

Tracy Plehn

very big and no way out that she could see. The door to the room was thick solid wood with iron bars for a small window.

The men had given her a blanket but it wasn't enough to warm her. Her fingernails were raw from tearing at the thick wooden door. Her hands, arms and legs were bloodstained from the wounds that had been inflicted by the men holding her captive. She had struggled with these men several times and each time they retaliated by punching and slapping the woman.

She cried a little longer then slid down the stone wall beside the door with her back until she hit the floor. Exhausted, she slumped down, her head hitting the floor then darkness enveloped her mind and she passed out.

I threw myself on the bed and decided to make an early night of it. Working double and triple shifts all these weeks was starting to wear on my body. I didn't fight it and gave in to sleep……..

I pulled into a driveway in a black pick-up. The driveway was not mine, the neighborhood either. The driveway was at a slight incline, cracked and led to a one car garage. The garage door was white, well dirty white and not completely attached, it hung crooked. The house it was attached to was small and brown; the paint chipping off from every angle of the outside I could see. It was a one-story house with a big window facing the same direction as the street. The window was cracked and had a long piece of silver duct tape holding it together. The front door was wide open, or was it missing....I couldn't tell at first. I walked to the front door but stopped before entering. I couldn't move; something wasn't right. I turned to look at the rest of the neighborhood and it was as run-down as this house. Most of the lawns were cluttered with cars, motorcycles, bicycles, toys, trash, etc.

Next thing I knew, I was in the living room. There was a small black and white TV in the corner across from the big window. The TV was on, I think it was a late night talk show but I couldn't make out which one. To the left of me was a gold and brown plaid couch under the big window that had the duct tape. On the other side of the couch was a metal folding table. The walls were dirty, probably white at one time and bare, no pictures hung anywhere I could see. The carpet of the house was olive green with cigarette burn holes throughout. I had stepped into the 1970's.

I walked into the kitchen ahead of me, well that was a mistake. Dishes covered the dull yellow counters; trash in and out of trash bags lay all over the floor and a metal folding table stood in the middle of the kitchen for a dining table. I couldn't stand it so I turned to the hallway that was to the right of the living room. As far as I could tell, there was only one level to this house, no basement.

I walked down the hallway, still no pictures on the walls. There was a bathroom on the right and a very small bedroom across from it. At the end of the hallway was another bedroom. Both bedrooms had nothing but stained twin mattresses on the floor, no frames. I walked to the first bedroom and opened the closet door. There was a full-length mirror on the inside of the door. I looked at the mirror, nothing too scary, just me looking back.

I closed the closet door and turned around but then a noise caught my attention. I did a half turn and realized the closet door came open again and I found myself looking into the mirror. It was me but not me this time. The image had my black hair in a military cut; the same square jaw line; blue eyes; dark complexion and my height of 6'2". I turned my head to the right and of course, the image in the mirror turned his. I drew my right hand up to the mirror and pointed my index finger on the glass. The image copied my movement but I knew something was different. It hit me, the face. I hadn't shaved in a couple days and the image was clean shaven!

I stood there shaking and looking into the mirror. Then the "image" stepped out of the mirror toward me! I wanted to jump out of my skin but luckily my skin stayed put and I froze. It, he, the image, whatever it was held up an envelope that read "Return to Sender" and placed it in my trembling hand!

I woke with a violent jerk, shaking and sweat pouring down my face and I could taste the salt. My pillow was soaked. I pulled my hand out from under the comforter and discovered an envelope that read 'Return to Sender' in my hand!

<u>TWO DAYS EARLIER</u>

Boulder, Colorado

It was June 3rd. I could tell it was going to be a long hot summer but also the start of some much needed time off. I'm a cop and had spent so many nights away in the last few weeks pulling double and triple shifts that I had almost forgotten where I lived but there it was, home sweet home.

After my dad died I moved back into the house I grew up in. I didn't have the heart to sell the house and have strangers living in it. It wasn't a huge house but it had been perfect for my dad, mom and me. The neighborhood was older and well established. The houses were mostly brick, lawns very tidy and everyone knew everyone's business.

I pressed the button on the remote control for the garage door and pulled my Ford F-150 into its usual spot. My dad had always kept the garage organized and I kept up the tradition. Between the two of us, I think we had every tool imaginable and every one of them neatly organized in large tool chests, 4 of them, standing along the wall of the garage. The other side of the garage was a work table that was half the length of the garage and shelves above it that my dad and I had built together. We had spent hours on the weekends working on our vehicles, bicycles or anything we could take apart and put back together. How I missed those days.

I strolled to the end of the driveway to retrieve my mail and it hit me. I have three weeks off! It had not sunk in until that very second and I was going to take the vacation of a lifetime well, my lifetime! I couldn't stop smiling after that realization and the neighbors probably thought I finally snapped. I took the mail into the house and laid it on the kitchen table. I decided to grab a Coke before plowing through the mail. I had been keeping up with the bills during these last few weeks but the rest of the mail got thrown into a pile on the table. UGH, what a mess!

I picked up what I had just thrown down and saw everything was junk except for one envelope. I held it out and threw the rest in the trash can I had dragged over to the table. This envelope had a return address from Georgia and was hand-written. I opened it up and pulled out a note that read:

>*"Dear Damien,*
>
>*It's been so long since we've seen other. I'm so sorry for the way I left. You really were starting to scare me and I didn't understand your work. I should have tried harder to understand and I know I left when you needed me the most. I hope and pray you can forgive me because I desperately need your help! I don't know what's going on but people are after me and I have no idea why. I'm at the same hotel in Savannah, where we stayed last year. Please contact me as soon as possible. I don't know how long I can hide before they find me. PLEASE HURRY!*
>
>*I still love you, Cassie"*

"Okay, that's weird. Sorry Cassie, I'm not Damien but I hope he made it to you in time. I'll send this back to you." I then realized I had said this out loud. I really have to get a life outside of work. I wrote 'Return to Sender' on the outside of the envelope and put it in the mailbox with the flag up.

I headed upstairs to take a shower and decided afterward I would be a complete vegetable for the rest of the night. I had not taken any time off work or had a vacation for five years and now I had the next three weeks off. I had so much time built up that I was told I would lose it if I didn't use it. They didn't have to tell me twice. I hadn't taken the time to figure out what I would do or where I would go but I would make that decision tomorrow. Making last minute plane and hotel reservations would cost more but that wouldn't stop me. I had been saving for a vacation for years and I would enjoy every penny.

The rest of my night consisted of reading in my favorite room of the house, the den that was off the entry way to the left of the front door. It had been my dad's favorite when I was growing up and I think that's why I loved it so much. I spent a lot of time playing cars and trucks on the floor in front of the giant brick fireplace while my dad would stretch out in the tan leather recliner reading his book. I guess it was actually a den/library as it had one whole wall from floor to ceiling with built in oak bookcases filled with every type of book imaginable. Another wall was covered with family pictures and my trophies from football and wrestling. In one corner of the room was my dad's big mahogany roll-top desk.

I made a fire then began reading. I must've been more exhausted than I thought because when I started reading it was about 8 in the evening. Next thing I knew it was 10:30, I had fallen asleep. I dragged myself out of the comfortable recliner and poured myself into bed.

I woke up the next morning with an inspiration, the Virgin Islands! I jumped out of bed, threw on some jeans and a blue t-shirt, ran down the stairs and called my travel agent. She made arrangements for me to leave in 3 days and spend 10 glorious days in St. Thomas. I daydreamed while on hold and could almost smell the salt water, see myself on the sandy beach drinking a....well, something with an umbrella in it. The girls in bikinis, tan, long legs.... that's what I'm talking about! Snorkeling and scuba diving.....this was the vacation I needed.

"Okay Mr. Reynolds, you're all set. I've got the first class flights, hotel and car all arranged. I'll have the tickets and itineraries delivered to you tomorrow. Will there be anything else?" The agent replied.

"Nope, I think that should do it unless you want to pack for me too. HaHa, bad joke." The agent pretended to chuckle then thanked me and we hung up. As soon as I put my cell phone on the kitchen table the doorbell rang.

"I know that can't be the delivery guy from the travel agency, she can't be that good." I opened the front door and it was a delivery man but not from the travel agency.

"I have an envelope for Mr. Reynolds." The guy said as he handed me a large brown envelope with my name and address hand written on the outside.

I signed the little electronic signature box he gave me.

"Thank you sir, have a great day."

"You too, thanks much." I took the brown envelope into the house. I pulled open the gooey flap and found a smaller envelope inside. To my dismay, it was the letter I returned to sender yesterday!

"What the hell? Maybe the mailman is pissed at me and decided to drive me crazy? I have GOT to stop talking to myself!" Then it dawned on me, Kenny who I've known since the Police Academy is a huge prankster, it had to be him. *But how would he have gotten the envelope? Saw me put it in the mailbox? That would mean he had been outside hiding and watched for me....okay, that's kinda creepy and I don't think he would even be that weird, that's borderline stalking.* As I thought this through I decided it wasn't Kenny doing a prank but I thought I'd call him and see what he thought.

Before calling Kenny I called the delivery company to see if they would tell me who hired them. I dialed the number I had noticed on the outside of the delivery van. I also realized that maybe I had been a cop too long, I noticed everything! What normal person notices a random number like that?

The lady was very kind on the other end of the line but she had no record of who sent it. She asked one of the guys who worked there and I heard him tell her that it showed up this morning shoved under the door with an envelope of cash to cover the delivery.

"Well, thank you ma'am you've been very helpful."

"I'm sorry I couldn't give you any other information." She told me to 'have a nice day' and hung up the phone. I dialed Kenny's number to get his opinion. Actually, I knew what Kenny would tell me, 'throw the damn thing away and go do some island chicks'.

"Hello?" It sounded like I woke him up.

"Hey dude, did I wake you up?"

"Um, that's okay what's going on?" Kenny said in a strained voice.

"I'm sorry, go back to sleep and I'll tell you about it later."

"No, that's okay, I gotta get up anyway. What's up man?

"Okay, I need your opinion about this weird thing that happened. I get this letter in the mail yesterday and when I opened it, it wasn't to me but some guy named Damien from a girl, Cassie, who needs this guy's help. It was addressed to me though. So I put it in the mailbox yesterday and wrote 'Return to Sender'. Just now, it was hand delivered to me!" I took a breath and waited for him to burst out laughing. He didn't.

"So who's Cassie, is she hot?"

"That's what I'm trying to tell you, I don't know. The envelope came regular mail addressed to me with my address but the letter inside was to 'Damien' and she said she was in danger and needed his help. She told him she's in the same hotel in Savannah, GA. and to please hurry. So I figured there was a huge mistake and I wanted to send it back so she knew she never got in touch with 'Damien'. I don't know what to do, toss it in the trash and forget about it?"

"I don't know what to tell you man. Maybe one of the slime balls you arrested is messing with you. Who'd you piss off?" Kenny started laughing.

"I didn't think about that, I hope not. I thought it might have been you but this is weird even for you. I'm just going to toss it and head to the islands. I'm going to St. Thomas in 3 days!"

"St. Thomas! You suck! You better bring me some island babe. Wait a minute, you're going to the islands and you're worried about some mishap in the Mail World?! Are you crazy? If this letter is a joke, I swear it wasn't me and you know I'd take credit especially since it's a good one. Forget that letter, throw it in the garbage and get your ass to the islands!" Kenny said while yawning.

"Man, I really am sorry I woke you up. Did you work graveyard shift last night?"

"Yeah, but it's alright because I have a ton of things to do today. Let's get in some tennis before we lose you to the islands."

"Okay, how about tomorrow? I'll make the reservation at the club and call you to confirm." I said the words but my mind was still drifting to the letter and who might be the culprit.

"Sounds good, talk to ya later."

I took his advice and threw the letter in the garbage, gathered up the bag and put it in garage. The rest of my day was spent running errands, shopping for tropical clothes and other necessities.

That evening after dinner I did the same as the evening before, took a shower and read the rest of the night. About 11:00 I threw myself on the bed and decided to make an early night of it. Working double and triple shifts all these weeks was starting to wear on my body. I didn't fight it and gave in to sleep......

Present Time (after the dream)

I couldn't stop trembling or catch my breath. When I was able to free my right hand from clutching the covers, I gathered every ounce of courage I had to take the envelope and lift the flap. I had taped the flap of the envelope before putting it back in the mailbox two days ago but there was no sign of tape. It was definitely the same envelope, my handwriting was on the outside that read 'Return to Sender', I also had just thrown it in the garbage last night AND put it in the garage! Did I sleepwalk and retrieve the letter out of the garbage? That had to be it but I had never done that before.

I started to throw the letter in the garbage once again. If I had gotten the letter out in my sleep then I would not have been in the frame of mind to secure the bag after retrieving the letter. But the trash in the garage was secure. I opened the bag and of course, the letter was not there. It would've been on the top. *Of course it's not there you bozo, you've got it in your hands.* I threw the letter in the trash once again.

I went upstairs and took a shower then did some cleaning around the house. The house cleaning had suffered a lot in the last few weeks. I couldn't find enough to do to keep my mind off that damn letter. I decided to take a break and head into the city. There was a sub shop on Pearl Street and their meatball sub, bread and sauce was to die for.

The shop was busy but I was not in a big hurry for once. Usually I stood in line when I was on duty and inevitably my radio would go off and I'd have to go. I was behind a nice looking young lady so at least the view was good. I was the last one in line and I turned around just as a guy about 25, my age, came tearing inside ahead of an older gentleman. He didn't even hold the door for the man. I was appalled and motioned for the older gentleman to get in front of me. He thought I was kidding and just stood there confused.

"Sir, it's okay. I'm not in a hurry and you can get in front of me." He slowly walked in front me smiling and the jerk who cut in front of him glared at me. I didn't care and tried to keep from losing my temper with him. My cell phone rang and I was glad for the distraction.

"Hey Jesse, I'm sorry for the incredible short notice but I can't make tennis today. Maybe we should shoot for when you get back. I got called into work again! I swear if they don't loosen their budget belts and get us some serious help we're all going to fall over dead. Anyway, have a fantastic trip and call me from the beach. Tell me in DETAIL what the island beauties are doing and wearing." Kenny said with a chuckle in his voice.

Crap, I completely forgot about tennis but this was perfect.

"That's okay, I actually have a lot to do to get ready for the trip. We'll make it another time. And don't worry, I'll give you every gory detail." We hung up and I decided not to tell Kenny about the dream and the physical evidence returning to me because he would've thought I was going crazy. I already decided I was nuts, why have my best friend confirm it?

I could still feel the guy behind me glaring. I tried very hard not to turn around and punch him. When the older gentleman finished ordering, he turned to me and smiled. I walked up to the counter to order.

I hurried back home and inhaled my lunch. By now it was one in the afternoon and I still had packing to do, then the doorbell rang. It was the travel agency's delivery of my tickets and itinerary. I thanked the gentleman and gave him a tip.

I went into my favorite room and sat in the recliner to look over the itinerary and make sure everything was in order. I did my best thinking in that room. I decided if the letter found me again I'd burn it.

Then it happened......I had a dream while I was awake! A dream, vision I don't know. My head began pounding and felt as if it would burst. Images whirled around. I grabbed both sides of my head and fell to my knees then the images took over....

I was in a big vehicle, black interior. I could tell it was an SUV. I was in front of a big building, barn maybe? I opened the driver's side door and stepped out onto gravel. My head turned to the front of the vehicle; it was a black Cadillac Escalade. I walked toward the open door of the barn and stopped. A gorgeous, no, gorgeous doesn't begin to describe her but this Goddess sat on a horse. It looked like she was in an indoor arena. She and the horse glided around the rails of the arena so smoothly I could've sworn they were one unit. Then I was sitting on the horse with her, I could smell the leather of the saddle, smell of hay and her shampoo; coconut. Her long black hair flowed around my face but it didn't bother me. The vision, or whatever this was, went outside and I stood looking around at the beauty of the landscape. I turned toward the barn and this

Goddess walked out in English riding clothes. I didn't know a thing about horses or riding but I'd seen some events on TV and she looked like one of the professional riders I'd seen and oh, so much prettier. She was graceful as she approached me and when she spoke, my heart melted. "Can I help you?" Well, that was a loaded question. What did she mean and what was I doing there? I didn't know if she could help me, I felt like I needed to help her.

It was over, my head stopped pounding. *What was that?!* I've never believed in ghosts, ESP, visions or anything of the supernatural but the oversized goose bumps on my arms were telling me something was happening. The back of my neck felt like a million tiny needles were pricking it.

I had this beautiful girl suddenly thrust into my life and I had no idea who she was. Her hair was black as night and hung all one length down to her waist. It was so straight and glistened like the sun shining on freshly laid snow. Her complexion was flawless, naturally tan, Hawaiian maybe. She was about 5'5" and very slender body. Her eyes, a light golden brown with speckles in them. They reminded me of the color ginger. My mom used that spice for cooking and the color matched this beauty's eyes. I wanted to keep her vision in my mind forever.

Without thinking, I grabbed my laptop and connected to the Internet. I Googled 'Savannah hotels' and typed in the physical address written on the envelope. I found it quickly. It was a bed and breakfast, and from the picture it looked like a plantation home. I wanted to call them and see if a 'Cassie' was there. *Hmm, I didn't have a last name for this Goddess. They're going to put me in the Funny Farm!*

"Good morning, The Olde Savannah Inn, may I help you?" The voice on the other end sounded like she couldn't be more than 12 years old but who was I to judge?

"I don't know. I'm looking for a lady with the first name of Cassie, I don't have a last name but I believe she's registered with you." The gal couldn't find Cassie's name on the Register. The best I could do was leave my name and number and she assured me she would call if she found anything out. I doubted she took me seriously and probably didn't even write my number down.

Now what? Do I forget the letter and the daydream, vision, whatever and go to the islands? Do I go on a wild goose chase and see if I can find Cassie? That's nuts, of course you go to St. Thomas. This whole thing is just proof that you need a vacation! Forget about it and go on vacation you idiot. I had talked myself into doing the logical, sane thing. I went into the living room and turned on the TV. I was just getting into a show when all of a sudden the 'vision' started again.

My head began to throb and each time this happened it sounded like thunder in my brain and the pain, I couldn't even describe it. My mind went black then a tornado of images until things settled into a vision...

I flashed to a car. It was a compact car, red with gray interior. I was driving on a long stretch of paved road. When I moved my head to look out the driver's window, it looked like a jerky, slow motion movie. There was nothing but thick green trees. I looked to the passenger seat and the Goddess was sitting there! The Hawaiian beauty spoke, the sweet peaceful voice of an angel. "We have to hurry; this is the only clue we have." She turned her head toward her window. She was gone.

I shook my head trying to rewind but my 'vision electronic equipment' was challenged. The rewind didn't respond so I had to try and bring the vision back by memory. I could still smell the coconut shampoo, so slight but so enticing. Wow! I decided I needed a shrink, not a vacation. It didn't matter, I was going to find a way to forget about the craziness and go to the islands. This was too insane to take seriously, I was losing my mind and maybe I'd find it in St. Thomas. Then the TV went snowy and my 'prickly feeling' on the back of my neck returned, again!

"HELP HER JESSE, DON'T HESITATE! Go to Bozeman, Montana as soon as possible!" It was a male voice that didn't politely tell me those words, it screamed. Okay, I was officially certifiable, freaked out and spooked all at once!

"Who are you?! What do you want from me?!!" I yelled but obviously no one answered me. The show I'd been watching returned to the screen. That did it; I knew I couldn't relax until I figured this mess out. Why Montana? What happened to the return address on the envelope in Savannah, GA? Did this voice from the TV know anything about American geography? Unless I would be intercepting Cassie before she got to Savannah and before she was in danger? Maybe the vision is the future. That made sense. I started laughing out loud when I thought that last sentence, 'made sense', nothing made sense.

I called my travel agent and changed my itinerary. I would fly out first thing tomorrow morning out of DIA to Billings, MT then rent a car to Bozeman. A wild goose chase and I was the idiot doing the chasing.

Chapter Two

Denver International was busy as usual. People walking fast while dragging luggage behind them; over their shoulders or hugging them to their chests. And families getting snippy with each other because of the long stressful day ahead of them. I stood in the 'First Class' line at Check-In. I didn't travel much but when I did I spent the extra money for the comfort and hopefully peace and quiet. I am a very private person and small talk with strangers was never my forte. I've been told I'm the 'strong silent' type, what does that mean? I'm not silent, I say what's on my mind. Oh well I am what I am.

I brought a black duffel bag filled with clothes and some toiletries that I would carry on. I didn't plan on this taking more than a day or so. I would then fly back to Boulder and pack for my real trip. The island would still be there in a couple of days. I stood there day dreaming, not visions this time, of the woman I hoped to see soon. I figured I could still dream about her even though her heart belonged to this 'Damien' person.

"Next in line please." The ticket agent seemed a little peeved that I didn't move the second she was free.

"Sorry, I was in another world." I said trying to cheer her up. It didn't work; she just gave me a fake smile and took my ticket.

"Okay Mr. Reynolds, you're all set. Please follow that hallway to Security….Next in line please." She didn't even give me time to thank her so I gathered my carry-on and ticket and walked away from the counter. The Security line was a mad house and I was relieved that I had plenty of time. My flight didn't leave for an hour and a half.

"Joey, knock it off….we will forget this trip and go home if you don't behave yourself!" A woman tried to say quietly but firmly behind me. I could tell she was frustrated and she caught me looking at her and little Joey. Her face turned red and apologetic.

"It's okay, I love kids. Hey Joey, do you like to play 'Cops and Robbers'?"

"Yeah, sometimes we just play cops. My daddy is a cop and sometimes he lets me turn on the siren." The little boy, I guessed about 5 years old, looked at me wide eyed with dark curls and big blue eyes.

"Hey, that's pretty cool and you know what? I'm a cop too! I think I have a badge in my bag, do you want it?" I asked Joey but finished the question looking at his mom for her approval. She nodded her head and gave me the 'thank you' look.

"Yeah! I'll make sure everyone on the plane is good and if they're not, I'll arrest them!" He reached out his hand eagerly; I placed the plastic badge in his palm.

"Okay Joey but the best way to be a cop is to listen, be very quiet and listen." I smiled at the mom and turned back around.

The line had moved only a couple of feet in that time. I pulled my real badge out of the duffel bag as I knew I would have to show it before my bag went through x-ray. I always carried my gun and not knowing what I was walking into in Bozeman I wanted to be extra careful. The girl from my 'vision' didn't seem to be dangerous but I had no idea what danger she may be in.

It was finally my turn and I took off my white tennis shoes and put them in the gray tub along with my watch and wallet. I had put my badge in my pocket and pulled it out to show the young TSA standing in front of me. I gave her my duffel bag so they could go through it and walked through the security post, buzzer free. I grabbed my tub, put my shoes back on, and gathered my stuff. I turned and waved good-bye to Joey and his mom.

I stopped at a newsstand/gift shop on the way to the gate to pick up a paper. I still had an hour until my flight left and the board indicated it would be leaving on time. I found my gate and sat in a chair facing the plane. I shoved my duffel bag between my feet and started to read the paper. It was full of the usual; homicides, rapes, burglaries, etc., too much gore for being on vacation.

Then Cassie's face popped into my head and I couldn't help but smile. I knew she belonged to Damien but I decided a little day dream about her now and then wouldn't hurt anything. I realized I must look like a doofus to everyone around me, smiling like a school boy. I'll be the one in the neighborhood all the moms will tell their children, "Stay away from Old Mr. Reynold's house! He sees things and hears voices in his head!" Yep, that will be me!

"We will now begin boarding Flight 4189 non-stop to Billings, MT. If you need assistance please let us know. We will start with rows 1-5." I glanced up when the attendant came over the intercom but all I could see was the small group of people heading to the line to give their boarding passes. I found my boarding pass, grabbed my duffel bag and headed to the line.

The line moved quickly and before I knew it, it was my turn.

"Thank you sir, you are seat 1A." A young blonde flight attendant took my boarding pass, ripped off her part and handed the remainder back to me.

"Thank you." I took my boarding pass and moved quickly to the plane.

I walked through the door and one of the other attendants stood at the entrance of the plane to greet us. I found my seat, shoved my duffel in the overhead and sat down.

The anticipation was beginning to overwhelm me. I had to get control of my senses and thoughts. I distracted myself by watching the passengers board the plane. Each person had the same look toward the person in front of them, 'hurry up; I want to get to my seat.' I got bored with that quickly and put the headphones from the seat pocket in my ears. I tuned into a station I liked and put my head back on the seat.

Montana

The trip to Montana was quick and easy. The wheels hit the ground of the runway and the engines made the agonizing sound of trying to slow the plane. We all lurched forward a little when the brakes started taking effect. We taxied a few minutes then came to a stop. The pilot had asked us to remain seated until the "Fasten Seat Belt" sign went off. The light dinged off and everyone on the plane instinctively knew what to do. I stood up and grabbed my duffel bag then patiently waited for the exit door to open.

Stepping into the gate area, I saw a lot of people with big smiles on their faces waiting for their loved ones and friends. I found the sign that read, "Baggage Claim, Rental Cars…" and headed in that direction. I stood outside and waited for the Alamo Rental Car van to take me to the rental lot.

I grabbed my bag when we arrived and walked up to the counter. The woman at the counter started with her spiel.

"Welcome to Alamo, may I help you?"

"Yes, I have a reservation under Reynolds." She immediately started typing into the computer.

"Oh, here you are. Hmmm…it looks like we had to change your vehicle though. You reserved a midsize and the one we had lined up for you hasn't been returned. It shows here that we are letting you take our SUV for the same price and we will fill your tank now and when you return. I'm so sorry for the inconvenience." The woman seemed concerned that I would make a scene, I felt bad for her. Little did this woman know, it was my 'destiny' to have an SUV and I would bet my next paycheck that it was black. This whole thing was becoming comical in a way.

"Not a problem at all. What kind and color is the SUV?" I asked the question but knew the answer.

"It's a black Cadillac Escalade. It's fully loaded with leather seats. I think you'll be happy with it. It actually gets decent gas mileage. Just sign here and I'll have Joe take you out and go over the workings with you. He'll also have you check it for any damage, dings, dents, etc." She took the contract after I signed, folded it and put into an Alamo envelope. "Keep this in the glove box; you'll need it when you return."

"Thank you." I flung the duffel bag over my shoulder. The woman at the counter pointed to a glass door and a man standing by a black vehicle.

I had picked up road maps before leaving Denver and mapped out the route, I was pretty sure I knew where I was going and didn't want to waste anymore time. Although, once reaching Bozeman I had no idea what to do. The TV voice or a 'vision' better happen by the time I get there. After inspecting the vehicle, I opened the door and climbed in. Joe told me to have a good trip and pointed me to the airport exit.

I found my way down the long winding hill that led away from the airport and into downtown Billings. Joe told me to stay on that street and it would take me directly to I-90. Once on the highway it was a straight shot to Bozeman. It didn't seem to be a very difficult drive and shouldn't take too long. I guessed about 2-1/2 hours. I stopped at Burger King before getting on the highway and grab something to eat and use the facilities.

It was only 9:30 in the morning so they were still serving breakfast. The line was kind of long so I went into the men's room first. I was the only one inside and as I opened the door my head began to pound again. I managed to reach the sink for support as I let the images swirl around in my head. The blackness turned into images of road signs...

I could see the signs clear as day and the last image led to a long dirt road. I was in the SUV driving down a road, I couldn't tell how far I would drive but it didn't seem too bad. The road abruptly ended into a driveway of a ranch.

I stopped the vehicle and read the brick arched sign that towered over the road, "Zamira's Dream Riding Academy", the initials ZD inside a cloud and under the initials was a horse head. You had to drive under the sign to continue down the driveway. The background was absolutely breathtaking. I couldn't tell how big the ranch was but the driveway went in two directions. To the right it curved to the front of a big two story log home and to the left looked as though it went to the barn. The front porch of the house seemed to be a wrap around with huge log pillars. The driveway was a red brick circular. In the middle of the circle was a beautiful fountain of a horse and rider, what a surprise.

I stared at the beauty for a few minutes then turned my attention to the barn; I assumed that's where I needed to find Cassie. The barn stood to the left of the house about 50 yards out. The road leading to the house was dirt then turned into the red brick but dirt again heading to the barn. I continued to the left in the direction of the barn. I parked the SUV off to the side of the barn door and got out. The barn was white, two story and gigantic. To the right of the barn was an outdoor small circular arena and to the left was a much larger outdoor arena. This ranch was nestled in a valley and behind it loomed magnificent mountains. Then the Goddess from my other vision walked out. "May I help you?" That voice was so angelic.

As usual, the vision stopped just when it was getting good. *Stop doing that and let me talk to this angel! Seriously, who are you and how do you plant this stuff in my brain?!* I yelled in my head, as if anyone would answer that would be too easy. I opened my eyes and was relieved to see no one had walked in while I was in the trance, maybe that's a better word for these weird visions. My head stopped pounding and I finished my business. I got my breakfast and had them bag it up for the road.

I was right; it took about 2-1/2 hours to reach Bozeman. I found all the road signs I needed to locate Zamira's Dream Riding Academy. I didn't even have to stop for directions. I went with it and let the images from my 'vision' guide me. There she was, just like the vision.

"May I help you?" I could listen to her voice all day and night.

"I'm not sure. My name is Jesse and I'm looking for Cassie." I hadn't even thought about my next move or words when she said she is Cassie. She's going to think I'm a scary insane guy when I tell her I received her letter, but the letter must've been from the future since she hadn't written it yet. Oh, this would be good. She'll be calling the local police to haul me away.

"Cassie? Who are you and why are you looking for my sister?" I could see her body language change and get defensive. Wait a second; did she just say 'sister'?

"Cassie is your sister?"

"I'm not telling you anything until you tell me who the heck you are." She tried to look mean but failed miserably. She was too cute to take on a mean stance.

I pulled out my badge and the letter Cassie wrote, I guess it wasn't from the future. I had to laugh inside at that. I was starting to sound as if all of this was everyday stuff and it happened to everyone all the time. I told her I wasn't here officially but I had received this letter by mistake and was having weird visions that led me to this ranch. I figured she'd turn around and run straight for the phone and call the guys with strait jackets.

"I'm really confused now and not sure why I'm here. I assumed it was to keep you away from danger but you're not even Cassie. I know I sound like a nut case and believe me, I've been feeling like I'm losing my mind. I'm normally a sane, logical person and nothing like this has ever happened to me before. Maybe someone is playing a practical joke on me but how your sister would be involved is beyond me. I've never seen either of you before in my life." I knew I was rambling but I needed to work this all out and somehow speaking it out loud helped. She stared at me for a long time before speaking.

"How do I know you're not some freaky stalker with a fake badge? You could've found out I had a sister on Google and wrote the letter yourself. How do I know you're telling me the truth?" She eyeballed me up and down then turned her eyes to the badge.

"You don't know. I can call my chief in Boulder and he can tell you I am a cop or better yet, call your local police and have them verify. I wouldn't blame you a bit and I would feel better if you at least knew I wasn't lying about that. The rest of it, I can't prove yet but I hope you let me." I gave her my cell phone. She took it but didn't take her eyes off of me. She didn't even look the number up and dialed the non-emergency number. She gave dispatch my badge number and put her on hold. She stood her ground staring at me while on hold.

"Okay, thank you Karen." She closed my phone and handed it back to me.

"Can I see the letter?" She reached out her hand and I put the letter gently in it. As she read the letter her ginger eyes began to tear up.

"We're identical twins. Now you're going to think I'm nuts but they say twins have a connection even when they're miles apart. I've had this strong feeling for a couple weeks that something was wrong. I haven't talked to my sister since she started dating this guy from Vegas, maybe a year ago. My parents talked to her a few months ago right after Christmas but nothing since. I've tried calling and writing but my cards have been sent back with "Return to Sender" written on them. Her phone must've been disconnected so I have no way of reaching her. I have no clue who this guy is that she's seeing or if she's even seeing him any longer."

"Well, first things first. Again, my name is Jesse Reynolds and it's very nice to meet you." I extended my right hand to her and she did the same with a firm hand shake.

"I'm Amanda but everyone calls me Mandy." She tried to smile but I could see the pain in her face and her eyes became sad instead of defensive. I tried to lighten the moment with a humorous discovery.

"So we have Mandy, Jesse and Cassie. Now we need someone whose name ends in a consonant. Okay sorry, bad joke." She hadn't heard my little joke and started back into the barn. I figured the best thing to do is follow. The barn was massive inside and out. The entry doors must be 15 feet high on metal runners that allow them to slide in opposite directions. One opens to the right and one to the left. Inside is a huge indoor arena, just like in the first 'vision', with white pole fencing. Lining the arena on either side were stalls, 12 on each side.

The stall doors were in two pieces so the top could be opened but the horses couldn't get out. As Mandy walked past each stall, horse heads immediately peered out to see what they might be missing. I was much clumsier walking past each stall as I was a little afraid of the huge heads lurking over the doors. One horse, about halfway down the breezeway, stuck his brown head as far over the door as possible trying to attach his mouth to my shoulder. I swung my shoulder away from his gaping mouth and heard a chuckle from a few feet away. I looked over my other shoulder to see Mandy chuckling at the contest between myself and this beast.

"Laugh it up funny girl. This horse is trying to have me for lunch. I didn't realize they eat meat." It was nice to see a full smile. She had a perfect, beautiful smile that lit up her entire face. It didn't last long as the smile returned to its sad state and I knew where her thoughts had gone.

"I need to turn some of the horses out to the pasture then we can go inside the house for some tea if you like."

"That would be nice. Would you like some help?" I forgot for a second that I was afraid of these beasts and realized I volunteered to help them out of their cages. I don't consider myself a weak, small man. I'm 6'2" and 210 lbs. and most of that is muscle but these 1000 lb. beasts scare me.

"That's okay. I appreciate it but I wouldn't want one of these beasts to nibble you to death. Meet me out front in a few." She half smiled again and put a halter on the horse that tried to eat my shoulder.

I gladly obliged and headed out to my vehicle. This gave me time to gather my thoughts and realize that the Goddess in my dream or vision or whatever was not Cassie and her heart didn't belong to this Damien dude. I wondered if she were married or had a boyfriend.

"I'm done; let's head up to the house." Mandy walked briskly past me and I caught a whiff of the coconut I smelled in the 'vision'. Then she stopped and turned to me.

"Jesse, we have to call the police again and show them the letter!" I guessed it was a delayed panicked urgency, I had expected this comment right after I showed her the letter.

"Well, I am the police and I did think about going to local authorities but what would we tell them? This letter showed up, I put it in the mailbox but it found its way back. I tossed it twice but it returned to me in a dream. I don't think they'd take us very seriously, I know I wouldn't if someone approached me about it. For now, we need to find out more." That seemed to appease her for the moment and we continued our way to the house.

The home was as beautiful inside as it was outside. The porch was a wrap around the entire home. The back door which faced the barn and the mountain scenery led into a humongous kitchen. The main level of the house was mainly open floor plan with high vaulted ceilings. A large island stood in the middle of this amazing room which was filled with stainless steel appliances, beautiful cherry wood cabinets and the counters were light colored granite. She poured some iced tea for the both of us and we took the glasses to the back porch. There were wicker chairs, 4 of them and a wicker coffee table to the left of the back door. To the right was a swinging bench chair with another wicker coffee table in front of it. There was another stand alone chair against the railing next to the swing and that's what I chose to sit in. Mandy sat in the swing and for a long moment we said nothing, she broke the silence.

"Tell me again about this letter and how you found me." The confusion in her face was indescribable. I told her every bizarre detail from beginning to end including the phone call to my buddy trying to get his opinion.

"I haven't gotten any more visions since Billings which led me to your door step. Trust me, nothing like this has ever happened to me before and I'm pretty freaked out about it. I have no idea on the next move, what I'm supposed to do or why I'm here. I'm seriously considering flying back home, packing my island clothes and start my real vacation but my gut is telling me to wait." I stopped and let her soak in the whole story.

"Can I see the letter and envelope again?" I had folded it and put in my short's pocket so I pulled it out again to show her. She read and re-read for several minutes.

"I think we need to go to this hotel or whatever it is in Savannah. Maybe the clerk or someone working there would remember Cassie. Maybe she's even there right now."

"I called already and they had no clue who she was. I didn't have a last name. The lady on the phone said they had no one with the first name of Cassie." I knew that wasn't what Mandy wanted to hear but I needed her know that may not be the best first step.

"I have to do something! Now that I know Cassie is in real trouble I can't sit around waiting. Jesse, what are we going to do?" More tears filled those beautiful ginger eyes as she handed the letter to me.

"I think we need to wait a little longer and see if I get another set of instructions. I don't know what to call these weird visions I'm getting but so far they're working. I never would have found you if I didn't decide to listen or do what they said." I heard the words come out of my mouth but it was still so surreal. I knew I couldn't question them any longer, just go with it and if my vacation was put out a few more days it would be worth it. Mandy was like a Hawaiian beauty queen and I could look into those eyes forever.

I wanted to keep her mind off of her sister for awhile so I asked about her life. She told me of her retired parents moving to Florida last year and Mandy stayed at the ranch. It was then that Mandy had called Cassie and asked if she wanted to help run the ranch but Cassie didn't want anything to do with the ranch. Cassie and her parents had been at odds for years and Cassie had quit high school when she was 17 and ran off to Vegas.

She informed Mandy of the guy she met a few months before that while working at the casino and she was madly in love. His name was Damien and that's all Mandy knew of him. She never met nor talked on the phone to him.

Mandy had gotten a degree in Social Work but decided to open this youth/riding academy. Her family moved to this place when the girls were two and she's never lived anywhere else. The girls were born in Hawaii but her parents wanted to raise them on the mainland. Her dad was a commercial airline pilot and her mom stayed at home with the kids. Mandy explained that the ranch had belonged to her grand-parents on her father's side. He grew up here as well but moved to Hawaii when he graduated high school. Mandy's parents met in Honolulu.

Both sides of their families are native Hawaiian and all moved mainland except the grand-parents on their mother's side. Her mother explained to the girls that her parents disowned her when she moved to Montana with Mandy's father. The girls never met their grand-parents on that side of the family. They died three years ago never knowing their daughter's two twin girls.

I found myself trying to keep my eyes from tearing. We had been sitting there for over an hour but it felt like seconds. Her voice was mesmerizing. We got interrupted by a woman running to the back porch.

"Mandy, I'm sorry to interrupt you but your next class will be here very soon." This woman was about 5'2", strawberry blond hair that was short and wispy and looked like it was naturally straight. She had a slender build, round face, very natural beauty. She kept one eye on me while she spoke to Mandy and I couldn't tell if she wanted to make sure I wouldn't chop them up into tiny pieces or steal Mandy away.

"Okay Becca I'll be right down. Oh, this is Jesse, Jesse this is Becca my secretary that I would be totally lost without. She runs this place, I just ride. "I caught a wink from Becca to Mandy and they had a look between them that only girls seem to know. I had given up trying to figure out that look between girl friends a long time ago. Guys do the "nod" of their heads when they approve of their friends' choice in girlfriends and may ask her why she's with this bozo. No reading minds or psycho analyzing the way girls do. We look at the girl's body, back to our guy friend and nod. If we don't approve then it's the ol' "it's nice to meet you" thrown in and a quick change of subject.

I had stood up when she came up the stairs and by now she was standing between me and Mandy. Becca shook my hand and smiled half at me and half at Mandy. She ran down the stairs and returned to the barn. Mandy made her apologies to me and asked if I'd be okay until her class was over.

"Of course, I'll be fine but do you mind if I watch?"

"I don't mind but are you sure you want to take a chance that the "beasts" might hurt you?" She winked and headed out to the barn.

Two cars pulled in beside my vehicle just as I was coming down the stairs. Four teenage girls bounded out of the vehicles giggling and tossing their hair. Thank goodness none of them noticed me as they raced into the barn. I meandered inside and found a chair placed out of the way by the front door. I wasn't sure if they would ride inside or out in that big arena. I sat in the chair while the girls and Mandy got their horses ready.

"Ms. Mandy you're riding Tobias today? Why not Zamira?" One of the young girls asked as Mandy came out of the stall with this really tall black horse. He looked as big as a building. How can that tiny woman get on this giant horse? I had to watch this.

"Tobias needs some exercise. I rode Zamira yesterday. Okay, girls we're going to the Dressage arena. Everyone meet me out in 3 minutes. Anyone not out in that time will work out bareback today." Mandy was really cute when she tried to be tough. The girls took her seriously though as they quieted down and concentrated on doing what people do before they ride these beasts.

Mandy walked past me with this black monster and I swear he gave me the evil eye. I must have had a goofy look on my face because Mandy busted up laughing, which was wonderful to hear. The horse swished its long black tail which proceeded to smack me in the face. I shook it off and followed way behind Mandy and the monster. I sat in the bleachers on the outside of the ring which would give me a view of the entire arena.

Mandy had pulled something out of her jacket pocket and I figured it was a treat for the beast but she put it in her own mouth. The beast tried taking it from her but she put it back in the pocket, came to the side of the animal and with one swift, graceful motion mounted this gigantic black building! I couldn't believe it! I had just met Mandy but she seemed really amazing so far. I couldn't keep my eyes off her as she moved with the horse around the arena. The four teenage girls came out of the barn all mounted on their steeds giggling again. One of the girls reached down from her horse and opened the gate to the arena for the other three to enter. If I had done that I would've fallen off and landed on my head.

"Girls I want some figure 8's to get your horses warmed up." Mandy yelled at the girls and they immediately did what she said. It was if Mandy had discovered a secret switch that turned teenagers into obedient vessels. Some parents would probably pay her a handsome amount of money for that trick.

Mandy came trotting, I think that's the term, over to the fence in front of the bleachers I sat in.

"You doing okay?" She asked me as she swung her monster's head toward the fence.

"I'm good. You look awesome out there and I can't believe how easy it was for you to get on that horse!" I was in awe with this woman but I was trying not to be so obvious about it, I didn't want her to think I was some creepy stalker dude.

"Well, this won't take long. After the girls leave we'll figure our next move and I'll ask Becca to cancel everything for awhile. I have a show coming up but it's not for a month so the lessons can wait." She swung the animal back around and continued the lesson with the girls.

Within minutes of Mandy returning to her lesson, my head began to pound and ache. *Give me some warning when you're about to invade my head!* I managed to get up and find my way under the bleachers so the girls wouldn't witness me freak out. It was always the same beginning, my mind went black, I couldn't hear or see anything around me then images would race or swirl through my head. It was as if someone pushed a fast forward button about 15 times then the images would turn into a vision or dream. This one was the worst one so far.....

"HELP ME!! Please, someone has to be out there! I'm down here, someone please..." It was a girl, woman maybe, I couldn't yet tell. Her voice was so hoarse from screaming and crying I guessed. The room that surrounded her was musty smelling, dark and cold. I was in the room with her, I couldn't get warm even though my physical surroundings was seventy-five degrees. The room looked like a wine cellar but all the wine holders were empty. It had stone walls and floors maybe 20'x20', not very big. The door to the room was thick solid wood with iron bars for a small window.

She had a blanket but it wasn't enough to warm her. Her fingernails were raw and her hands, arms and legs were bloodstained. She cried a little longer then slid down the stone wall beside the door with her back until she hit the floor. I tried to reach for her but she couldn't see me. I couldn't see her face. She slumped down, her head hit the floor then she passed out. I walked over to her and I wanted to reach down and take her out of this hell hole but I could do nothing. I looked at her face and it was Mandy's face! NO! It can't be!

The vision stopped as suddenly as it began. The visions always stopped quickly, it made my head spin. *Was this a vision of her sister or is this a future happening to Mandy? I don't want it to be either!* I thought to myself. I never knew how long I was in these trances but when I became fully aware of my surroundings I realized the lesson was still going on but Mandy had noticed me and was trying to act like she hadn't. It didn't seem as though the girls saw me, thank goodness. How do you explain to a teenage girl that your brain has become entangled in a web of images you can't control? That would go over well. All their parents would have me committed.

Mandy spoke to the girls to keep them moving but she had an eye on me. I knew there would be explaining to do but I didn't want to scare her. I wasn't even sure if it was her or Cassie. I'd have to think fast because she was wrapping up the lesson and would be out soon. *Think Jesse. I think I'll just say that I had a vision but it didn't make any sense and I have no idea what it was. She'll buy that, she doesn't know me well enough to know that I'm keeping something from her.* I had it all worked out in my head but delivering it out loud might be another story. I was horrible at lying even if it was for someone's own good.

All the girls came piling out of the arena and headed to the barn. Some guy came out to meet Mandy and took her horse from her. Great, that means I have to explain that much sooner.

"I'll be right back. I'm going to find Becca and have her cancel upcoming lessons for a few days." Mandy yelled at me but kept her eyes on me as she walked to the barn. I decided to stay put and rehearse my well, lie. I rubbed my temples to help rid my headache quicker. They usually subsided seconds after the visions but not this time. Listen to me; I act like I've had these my whole life.

"Jesse, are you okay? What happened? Did you have another vision? Jesse, is it about my sister?" I kept rubbing my temples trying to get the courage to lie and Mandy was getting more impatient by the second.

"I don't know what it was. The pictures were all jumbled and I couldn't make it out." I tried to be convincing.

"I don't believe you. Jesse, you're not telling me everything. What did you see?" Her face was tight and her body language was turning angry. She clenched her jaw and fists.

"Are you going to punch me? I swear I couldn't make anything out of this one. The last three were clear as a bell with no question." I knew the routine when interrogating a suspect and I knew the signs to look for in a lying suspect. I felt I covered myself fairly well but I couldn't be sure.

"I'm gonna punch you if you don't tell me exactly what you saw! Please Jesse, I have to know." Her anger was quickly turning to fear.

"Okay, okay. I'm still not sure what it means. I saw a room, some sort of wine cellar. It was dark and cold." I still didn't want to say the whole truth about seeing Cassie or it might have been Mandy in the future and that scared me more. It seemed like Mandy wasn't breathing while she listened to me. Looking into those eyes made it much tougher not saying the whole truth. I also knew she would be more confused and terrified if I told her.

"Mandy are you alright?" The guy that took Mandy's horse to the barn came running to the bleachers.

"I'm fine Tony. Thank you. This is Jesse and Jesse this is Tony, my barn manager. Between him and Becca this place would simply be a house and barn." I extended my hand to Tony but he looked me up and down and would not extend his. I was relieved that she had a protector around her. He slowly walked to the barn, watching me the entire time.

"I'm sorry about that, he's very protective." Mandy informed me as she looked at the ground swishing her foot in the dirt.

"It's okay; I'd be the same way with you and Becca. Mandy, I don't know what else to tell you. I'm very new to this whole 'vision' thing and I can't control them. I don't think we should make another move until I have some more information." Mandy sighed and seemed to accept my explanation.

"Do you have a place to stay until we know where we're going?"

"I hadn't even thought about that but I saw some hotels in town. I'm sure they have rooms available."

"I doubt it. It's the beginning of summer and they're usually booked all season. I have lots of room so you're welcome to stay here." She started walking toward the house and I followed her.

"That's really nice Mandy, thank you. I can help out around here; let me know what I can do. I promise as soon as I know what direction we should go, I'll tell you."

"Why do you think I want you to stay here? I don't want you leaving without me, that's my sister out there somewhere." She half smiled and walked into the house and I was right behind her.

"Follow me and I'll show you your room." She showed me where the bathroom was, clean towels and the guest room I would occupy. This house was unbelievable and filled with family pictures and horse trophies from the girls. The guest room where I would sleep had a four poster queen size bed; hunter green comforter and drapes; and cherry wood dresser and chest of drawers. The bed was placed under a window that looked out the side of the house with a view of the mountains. A large antique trunk lay at the foot of the bed filled with blankets and pillows. This was much better than a hotel room and the company wasn't bad either.

She left me alone while I gathered my duffel bag from the car and took a shower. When I returned to the kitchen after the shower she had dinner on the table.

"I think Becca feels sorry for me and makes a week's worth of dinners for me to freeze. I've asked her to stop but then she makes more so I've given up and enjoy the food. She's a fantastic cook. She knows if she left it up to me I'd live on mac and cheese meals. I can barely boil water."

After dinner we retired to the "sitting room" and drank some wine and talked for hours. Before we knew it, it was midnight! Neither of us could believe how fast the time flew. Tony had come up to the house before he left for the evening to say good-bye. I knew his agenda, to make sure Mandy hadn't been chopped up into tiny pieces.

Mandy and I went to our separate rooms and said good night. I knew I'd sleep like a baby and hopefully things would be clear in the morning. I stripped down to my boxers and hopped into bed. The bed was amazing; it was like jumping onto thousands of cotton balls. It didn't take long to fall into a deep sleep.....

It was the vision from earlier in the red compact car with Mandy but with a little more detail. I was driving on a long stretch of paved road. This time when I moved my head to look out the driver's window I saw signs evident of Georgia. I turned my head forward to the windshield and a big sign that read "Welcome to Savannah" loomed in front of us. That's when Mandy said, "We have to hurry, this is the only clue we have." She was holding Cassie's letter to her chest. The images disappeared and I sat straight up. I felt like I'd been asleep for hours but when I looked at the clock it had only been an hour and a half since I climbed into bed. I lay back down and decided to wait until morning before telling Mandy what the next move is. She had been right and the next move would be Savannah, Georgia. I knew she was stressed and exhausted, she needed sleep before our long journey.

As I lie there, I debated whether to leave without her and find Cassie on my own or wait. Not knowing what danger lie ahead and what type of people were after Cassie worried me tremendously. I also thought it would be safer for her to be with me since the danger might discover Mandy exists and come after her. I decided to take her with me, besides she would probably hunt me down if I left on my own.

I didn't get much sleep after the vision but I felt good when 7:30 rolled around. I climbed out of the comfortable bed, my feet hitting the soft rug which felt great. I decided to take a shower before heading down stairs but the smell of coffee hit my nose and that changed my plan momentarily.

Mandy was in the kitchen attempting to make some eggs and bacon for us and the aroma filled the whole room. She was struggling with it but she tried. I stood there a few moments until she caught me staring at her. I never ate breakfast but I would definitely make an exception today.

"How did you sleep?" Mandy asked as she continued with breakfast.

"Fantastic. That bed is unbelievable, thank you." I stood at the island in the middle of the kitchen and poured myself a cup of coffee. Mandy had put two coffee mugs on the counter for us, coffee I never turned down. The mugs were big, a light brown clay with the ranch's logo on them. I decided to tell her about the vision and see how she felt about going to Savannah today. After I explained her mood seem to go from forlorn to "let's go now!"

"Absolutely! When do we leave?" She forgot she had been stirring the scrambled eggs and when the eggs began to turn a darker brown she wheeled around to the stove to save them.

"I'm going to hop on the Internet and get us lined up then I'll take a shower if that's okay."

"Of course. I'll arrange things with Tony and Becca then pack for the trip." She was obviously anxious and happy to finally do something to find her sister.

Chapter Three

The best I could do out of Billings was a 3:50pm flight to Salt Lake City and from there we'd connect to a flight to Hartsfield International Airport in Atlanta, Georgia. We wouldn't get into Georgia until close to midnight. I had made reservations at a hotel close to the airport for the night then we would go to Savannah first thing in the morning. I had called Alamo and made arrangements to have the car ready when we landed in Georgia, that way we wouldn't have to waste time in the morning. I didn't specify what color vehicle but I guessed it would be a red compact with gray interior.

Mandy and I got on the road around noon since it was only a two hour drive to Billings. I returned the SUV then we found our way to the gate. By that time we had 45 minutes until the flight left so we sat down and talked. As usual, time flew while listening to her voice. Mandy's ginger colored eyes glistened as she told me more about the kids at the ranch. She was very passionate about her work. She had pulled out a bag of Skittles while we talked and I finally asked her if that's what she had in her pocket at the ranch. I had noticed she pulled something out after riding. She confessed that those were her only bad habit. She loved Skittles and always had a bag of them with her.

"Okay Skittles, they're calling our flight." I grinned at her and decided that would be my nickname for her.

"Skittles? Fine smarty pants, I'll figure out your Achilles Heel." She winked at me as she gathered her bag. I didn't want to tell her what my nickname was at work, Scooby. Kenny discovered how obsessed I was with Scooby Doo and that became my nickname. I'd keep that under wraps.

Georgia

The flight to Salt Lake was uneventful as was the flight to Atlanta. It had been a very long day and luckily, the car rental company had the car ready and waiting. A red compact car with gray interior, go figure. I had to laugh a little as I signed the paperwork; we grabbed our carry-on bags and went straight to the hotel.

The rooms were decent and they put us next door to each other. I told the clerk downstairs to give us a 6 am wake up call. I had already made a reservation for us at the The Olde Savannah Inn which is the origin of the letter so I had nothing to do but slip into bed. It wasn't as comfortable as Mandy's guest room bed but it would do.

The phone rang at 6 am and it felt like I had just fallen asleep. I hopped in the shower, threw on some clothes and gathered my belongings. Mandy was in the hallway about to knock on my door when I opened it. We startled each other and laughed.

We loaded up the car after checking out of the hotel and got on the road. We found our way to Highway 75 heading south and we would connect with I-16 to Savannah, about a four hour drive.

We were both silent for most of the trip. I was trying to get a game plan together in my head for finding her sister and still pondering the questions, 'why me? What did I have to do with this?' I decided to just go with it and think of it as helping out a damsel in distress.

After three hours of driving I was beginning to get a little tired but we were only an hour away so I kept pushing on. Mandy had not said more than five words since we left Atlanta. I knew she was very worried about her sister so I didn't take it personally. The last hour of the trip went by quickly and uneventful.

The next exit should be, according to MapQuest, where The Olde Savannah Inn is located. As we got closer to the exit the sign for the hotel gave a general direction that I followed willingly. I pulled the vehicle in front of the door and Mandy came in with me. The man at the front desk was very helpful and friendly. He had blonde hair, light brown eyes and muscular build. He handed me the paperwork and keys for two rooms. Mandy tried to push my hand back when I gave him my credit card.

"Jesse, I'm paying for this! You're here to help me and it's not right for you to pay anything." I gently moved her hand back.

"You can pay the next one." I said it to make her feel better but I had no intention of letting her pay for anything. She gave me the 'whatever' look and half smiled. The man at the counter quietly laughed at us.

"Your rooms are one floor up and to the left, first rooms on the right. Dinner is at 6:00 and tonight is your choice of salmon or pork roast. Breakfast starts at 6:00am to 9. Please do not hesitate to call if you need anything." The gentleman handed us the keys with a big smile on his face. I could tell he had a question for us but seemed embarrassed to ask. I decided to make the first move.

"Actually, I wondered if you've seen a woman that looks exactly like this beautiful woman?" I put my arm on Mandy's shoulder.

"Yes, I'm sorry I was staring but the resemblance is remarkable. Your twin sister perhaps?" He looked very relieved that I got the question out in the open.

"Please, tell me when you saw her last! I'm very worried that something may have happened." Mandy's eyes widened with the possible hope of someone, anyone knowing where Cassie may be.

"It's been a few days since I saw her. I'm not supposed to do this but I can at least tell you when she checked out." He started typing on the computer then looked at Mandy. "Looks like she checked out June 1st. She seemed anxious and when I asked if everything was okay she just nodded, paid for her room and left. I watched her leave and was a little worried about her driving. She was parked out front and two men were standing by her car. I went out to make sure she wasn't in danger but by the time I got out there she had gotten in the driver's seat with the two men in the car and sped out of the parking lot. I assumed they were friends." He stared at Mandy the entire time and it was apparent he wished he'd taken other measures with Cassie, maybe call the police.

I thanked him for the information. Obviously we weren't getting much information from this place but it was a starting point. I didn't know what to do from here and decided a good night's sleep would help us both. We found our rooms and I gave Mandy the choice of which one she wanted.

"I'm going to shower then how about we go downstairs and have some dinner? You must be starving by now." I had realized that all we both had to eat today was snacks from the plane yesterday!

"That sounds great. Just knock on the door when you're ready." We both went into our rooms and it was a relief not to be moving any longer. Between flying and driving, my head was screaming for 'no more movement'. I took a long hot shower then changed into shorts and a t-shirt.

I knocked on Mandy's door but she didn't answer. I wasn't sure if I should be persistent or give it a little longer. Had she fallen asleep? I really didn't want to wake her but what if something happened and she was in danger. I decided to give it a few more minutes then try again. I turned on the TV and channel surfed before settling on the local news channel. I must've fallen asleep because

I was startled by a knocking noise. I looked at the clock and it said 7:30!

"I'm coming!" I jumped up and opened the door to find Mandy standing there just as gorgeous as when I'd left her awhile ago. She had changed into shorts and a t-shirt as well and those legs. *Knock it off Jesse, stay focused.*

"I wasn't sure if you fell asleep and I didn't want to wake you but I'm hungry and knew you must be as well." She was looking at her feet while she spoke.

"No, that's okay. I'm so sorry. I knocked a little while ago and thought you must've fallen asleep and I was only going to wait a few minutes but sleep got the best of me. Let's go get some grub. I guess we better go into town, they're done with dinner here." I gently took her elbow and nudged her forward.

We found a little seafood place not far from the Inn and sat at a table close to a window. The view was magnificent. The waitress brought us menus and two glasses of water.

"I'll be back in a few minutes for your order." She was sort of plain looking but not ugly. Her hair was thin, black and pulled into a bun behind her head. She was very skinny and not very tall, 5'2" maybe and very soft spoken. I imagined she was very shy and kept to herself outside of work. She wore wire framed glasses that must've been too big because she had to push them back a couple times just in the 30 seconds she stood there.

We sat looking at our menus and I decided fairly quickly. I folded my menu and set it on the edge of the table.

Mandy still stared at hers but I noticed that her eyes weren't moving.

"Are you okay?"

"Um oh, yeah I'm sorry. I was just thinking." She folded her menu and set it on top of mine.

"Aren't you hungry? You should eat something. We haven't eaten since yesterday."

"No, I'm not hungry but I'll get a shrimp salad." She still looked lost in thought so I left her to her thoughts.

Mandy's attention was suddenly distracted and she jumped up, nearly knocking over her chair. I was about to ask what was going on when I saw the kindness in her coming out in full force. A woman in a blue dress and high heels had walked out of the bathroom with the back of her dress hiked up into her panty hose. Mandy got to her before she rounded a corner where anyone else would've noticed. Mandy whispered to her and the woman, obviously embarrassed, backed up to the wall next to her and pulled her dress down. She gently touched Mandy's arm and I could see her mouth 'thank you so much' to Mandy. The woman stood there a few seconds to collect herself, her face was beat red.

I was in awe and could barely breathe. Mandy came back to the table and sat down. Here was a woman that was terrified her sister may be dead, travelling with a total stranger, not sure if she or the stranger will live and she still helps a woman from embarrassing herself in front of whomever she came to the restaurant with.

I couldn't speak. I just stared at this amazing person sitting across from me that I had met only hours before. The emotions going through me were those of knowing someone for years. I had only been close to 'Love' one other time, four years ago, but never in the year and a half we were together did I feel such yearning or admiration for another individual. Mandy was truly an angel. That was the moment that I knew I was completely at her mercy and she didn't even know it.

I reached across the table and took both of her hands in mine. She slowly looked up and we both stared into each other's eyes. I never wanted this moment to end. It did.

"Are you ready to order?" The waitress snapped both Mandy and I back to reality and we released our hands.

"Yes, I believe so." I looked at Mandy.

"I will have the Shrimp Salad with Ranch Dressing on the side please."

"And for you sir?"

"The Seafood Platter please."

"What kind of dressing for your salad?"

"Ranch as well."

"Those will be up shortly." She put her pen back into the pocket of her apron and spun around to the kitchen.

"Jesse, do you think this is some wild goose chase? Someone playing a sick joke on us?" She stared again into my eyes. I never wanted to see those eyes sad or hurt.

"I don't think so. How could anyone plant visions into my head and what would I have to do with this? If it was a sick joke it would have to be someone that knew both of us and what are the odds of that? I am starting to believe, well kind of, that there may be another realm to our universe and though I haven't figured out how you and I are tied to this mystery, I think it definitely has to do with finding your sister alive and well."

"I hope you're right." She looked down at my hands and took them in hers. She did that half; it was actually more of a quarter smile that she had managed throughout the day.

We got our food and ate in silence. Mandy ate most of her salad and I decided it was better than nothing so I wouldn't bug her about eating more. The waitress asked if we needed anything else and I shook my head. She gave us the check and we headed to the cash register. I went back to the table to leave the tip after I got my change from dinner.

I put my hand on the small of Mandy's back to guide her toward the door. We drove in silence the few minutes returning to the Inn. We stood in front of Mandy's door in silence for a few seconds staring down at our hands that were intertwined.

"Mandy, if you need anything tonight, knock on the door okay? I don't care what time it is." I took her key and unlocked her door.

"Thanks Jesse and thank you for being here, going through this with me." She gave me a hug then stepped into her room and shut the door. I did the same.

I channel surfed again and found my favorite show, Scooby Doo cartoon. I lay there on top of the comforter, still fully dressed staring at the ceiling. My mind wandered to Mandy, as usual and couldn't even enjoy the cartoon but I sure enjoyed the images of her. I heard a quiet knock on the door. I jumped up and opened it.

"Did I wake you? I'm so sorry if I did." Mandy stood in the hallway shaking.

"No, not at all. I was just watching my favorite cartoon. Yes, I said cartoon." I tried lightening the mood but could see she was upset. Of course she's upset you dolt, her sister's missing.

"What's wrong, are you okay?"

"I had a nightmare and I can't go back to sleep. I was wondering, if you don't mind....well, if I could stay in here with you?" Of course being a typical male, my mind started having all sorts of fantasies in the two seconds it took me to answer her. Being a civilized man, I knew all she needed was to be held and made to believe everything would be okay. That's exactly what I would give her. She deserved anything her heart desired.

"Absolutely, I would enjoy the company." I didn't want her uncomfortable so I grabbed a blanket that was folded in the little closet area and spread it out over the bed. She pulled one corner up and crawled underneath it. I came around the other side and climbed underneath with her. I laid on my back and put my arm around her shoulders, gently pulled her next to me to reassure her that I expected nothing, just sleep. She didn't hesitate and followed my lead. She lay on her side with her head on my chest and her right arm draped over my stomach.

I kept my right arm over her shoulder and brought my left arm down to rest on hers. This felt very natural. Her skin was so soft and I really had to control myself.

"You like Scooby Doo huh?"

"It's been my favorite since I was a kid. I would watch it every Saturday morning after my chores." She chuckled a little then I felt her entire body relax.

Morning came too soon but there was no time to waste. I had a really strange feeling about today but I didn't want to say anything to Mandy. She'd either think I was crazy or she would get scared. I couldn't put my finger on the 'feeling.' I hadn't had any visions or dreams it was just a feeling this time. Mandy was sleeping so peacefully and I didn't want to wake her. I stared at her peaceful, beautiful face for a minute. Her breathing was even, her facial expression relaxed like she didn't have a care in the world. I wasn't sure if she would stay in my life, I hoped so, but she was in it now and I would do anything to keep her safe and find her sister.

I gently pulled my arm from under her head, it was partially numb and had a tingling feel to it but I didn't care. My arm could've fallen off from her laying on it and I still would've been happy. I jumped in the shower and threw on another pair of shorts and a t-shirt then decided I better wake her up.

I walked into the room and realized the bed was empty. My blood ran cold and sent a chill up and down my spine. I could feel panic run through my body....then I saw her from my peripheral vision standing on the balcony. The room faced east so the sun was shining brightly on her. Her hair shimmered silver streaks in all the blackness and waved slightly in the breeze. Mandy had her face to the sun and both hands on the railing. She looked like a statue of a Greek Goddess.

I opened the sliding glass door quietly and stepped out with her. I couldn't believe how relieved I was that she was here and safe. Could I be falling for her, I just met her? I kept asking myself that question over and over. Could there really be such a thing as your "soul mate" and she was mine? But if she were mine, did she know that meant I was hers? Is there such a thing as "love at first sight"? I knew I would drive myself insane with all these questions. *Focus Jesse, go with it and get the task done in front of us first then figure out the rest.*

I put my hands around her small waist and pulled myself a little closer to her. I could smell the coconut in her hair from her shampoo. I was worried that she would slap me but decided to take the chance anyway. To my surprise and enjoyment, she didn't even flinch. She pressed her body against mine in response and tilted her head toward my chest. My chin came to the top of her head and I rested it there for a few seconds until she turned to face me. I kept my hands on her waist as she turned and she put her hands on my arms.

She slowly looked up at me and we stared into each other's eyes for several long moments. I could see her soul through those auburn eyes; it was so gentle, so vulnerable. She had her teeth on her bottom lip as if she were trying to hold herself back. I leaned in then hesitated one inch from her and stared into those eyes again. She leaned up the rest of the way and closed her eyes. I closed my eyes and tilted my head to the right ever so slightly and our lips touched. She let out a little sigh then pulled her head away. I opened my eyes. Her eyes darted back and forth slowly from one side to the other looking into mine.

"What do we do now Jesse? What if this is a complete dead-end?"

"I'm not sure but we better stay here until something, vision, whatever happens to me tells us what to do next." Listen to me, I sound like a lunatic.

"Jesse, what if.....what if she's....dead?"

"We can't think that way." I just hoped this wasn't a wild goose chase. What was I saying, of course it was! We were relying on visions for crying out loud to guide us to her sister! We walked back into the room and decided to have some breakfast downstairs.

It was a nice dining area, very homey. We sat at a little round table by the window that overlooked the beautifully lush landscape of the inn. The table was covered with a light green floral pattern table cloth. It was set with maroon plates, silver ware and coffee cups that matched the plates. The waitress walked to our table with two glasses of ice water.

"Would you like some coffee or juice?"

"Orange juice for me." Mandy answered then turned to me

"The same please."

"I'll bring those right out. Help yourselves to the buffet." She smiled at both of us and walked away.

We both headed for the buffet and filled our plates with scrambled eggs, bacon and muffins. I was very happy to see Mandy with an appetite. We sat down and ate our meals in silence. As we finished eating Mandy broke the silence.

"So Scooby, you're a cop?"

"Yes Skittles, I am." We both laughed at the nicknames.

"I suppose you could say it's in my blood. I'm a 4th generation cop. My dad, his dad, and so on. I don't really think I had a choice in the matter. There was never a question in my mind what I was meant to do with my life."

"Is your dad still on the Force?" I could tell she was trying to take her mind off her sister and the danger we were both heading into. I obliged without hesitation.

"My dad died three years ago on the job by a convenient store robbery gone badly. The guy that shot my dad was in the getaway car and saw my dad go to the door of the store. He shot him before he entered and my dad died instantly. I wasn't on duty that day but I heard the call on the scanner and knew instantly which cop was down. The shooter ran into the store to get his counterpart and was shot and killed by his own buddy. Luckily the second shooter will never see the outside of his cell."

"I'm so sorry. I can't even imagine what that must've put you through. What about your mom?"

"My mother died in a car accident when I was four years old so I don't remember her. My dad talked about her and told me stories repeatedly. There were tons of pictures of her throughout the house and in photo albums and my dad made sure I looked at them all the time so I wouldn't forget everything. I could tell that my parents were more than in-love; they were each other's entire lives so it didn't surprise me that my dad never re-married. There were times I would find him in his study sitting in the recliner staring into space. He never really got over her death." I could picture him so clearly in that memory.

"Wow, you've had a lot of tragedy in your life." She had tears trailing down her cheeks. I squeezed her hand.

"Yeah, it was a long time ago."

"Do you have someone special in your life back home?" She looked a little embarrassed.

"Not anymore. We broke up about a year and a half ago. I think it mainly has to do with my job. Not many girls want to put up with the long hours and wondering if I will come home after my shift. I thought I was in love, we were even engaged but she said she couldn't handle me being a cop. Looking back on it, I realized I was in love with the idea of being in love."

"Yeah, I can definitely see where she would worry....a lot." Mandy left it at that and then it dawned on me. If she ever started to care for me, she would start worrying as well. Would we be able to have a future? I could actually put myself in someone else's shoes this time because I am extremely worried about the danger we're heading into. It's not my safety I'm even considering but Mandy's. I don't think I would survive if anything happened to her, ever. At the same time, if something happened to me, I could not keep her safe. I was going to have to be extra careful.

"Can I get you anything else?" The waitress returned and I did notice that she had interrupted us several times but she was always friendly so I didn't think anything of it. I did notice Mandy chuckling.

"Yes, refills on our drinks."

"I'll be right back." The waitress walked back to the kitchen.

"What?" I couldn't imagine what I had said or maybe she had just thought of something funny.

"Are you that oblivious?" She smiled completely this time and her smile just lit the entire restaurant. It was dazzling, her whole face especially her eyes, lit up the room. I had to find a way to see that more often. I didn't know this angel but I knew out of anyone on this planet, she deserved to smile and be happy.

"Oblivious to what?" I honestly had no idea what she was talking about.

"The waitress has been totally flirting with you." She giggled and turned to the window.

"I think I would know if someone's flirting with me and she definitely was not." I didn't realize that came out as a sort of dare.

"Really? You would know if a strange woman flirted with you? Everyone is that obvious?"

"Yes they are." I squeezed her hand gently and let go to take the drinks from the young lady now standing to my side.

"Thank you very much." I tried to pay attention to the so-called flirting but just didn't see it until she winked at me.

"Just let me know if there's ANYTHING else you would like." She turned back to the kitchen and I heard the other waitresses giggling. Then on my napkin I noticed she wrote her name and phone number. This time it wasn't a chuckle that came out of Mandy's adorable mouth but a full blown laugh. Even though her complexion was dark, I could tell she was blushing. Her laugh had embarrassed her and she covered her mouth with her hand and tried to contain herself.

It then occurred to me that this waitress must not be as innocent as I suspected. She had to have seen Mandy and I holding hands! She didn't know if we were dating or married. I realized that she was quite the little vixen.

"Laugh it up funny girl! Okay, this time my radar was way off but I'm not to blame. I have the most beautiful girl sitting across from me and you expect me to notice another woman? You're kidding right?" We both laughed and sipped on our drinks. We sat in silence a little while staring at each other. I really could stare into those eyes forever, longer than forever. The waitress came back one more time but I looked at my watch and realized we had been sitting there for over two hours.

"No, we're done. Can we have the check please?" She noticed the napkin on the table with her number crumpled up, that stopped the flirting and now she seemed embarrassed.

"Yes sir." She quickly reached into her apron pocket and laid it on the table in front of me.

Mandy and I got up and headed to the register. I paid the check then put a tip on the table. We decided to go into town and window shop. I hoped that would kill some time while we waited for whatever it was to invade my head with our next move. It still baffled me as to who if it was a 'who', was giving me these 'instructions'.

We drove into the city and I parked in front of the first shop Mandy wanted to see. We decided to walk up and down each side to see all the shops. We started into the shop when my head began to implode. I could barely get any words out and I didn't want to scare her but I needed her to help me get out of the public eye.

"Mandy, there's an alley behind us. Please help me over there." I grabbed my temples and tried to keep my head from exploding. I knew she was scared but there was nothing I could do. I didn't know if we made it out of the public's view because as usual, my mind went black and I could hear or see nothing. The images stopped swirling and settled....

"I hope you enjoyed your flight and welcome to Las Vegas ladies and gentlemen. Please wait until the 'seatbelt' signs are turned off before moving around the cabin. Enjoy your stay." I walked off the plane and looked to my right; I was holding Mandy's hand while we walked quickly. She was still with me and safe, thank goodness. We were both in different clothes and I had our duffel bags on my shoulder. We stopped at a car rental agency, of course we did! Well, what type of vehicle this time? My question was answered quickly as we were in a black pick-up on the on-ramp to the highway. We exited and I couldn't see the name of the exit but there was a large sign for Motel 6 to the right of us just off the highway.

"We'll stop here and ask for directions." I looked at Mandy as I said this. We had been holding hands on top of the console. I let go of her hand and went inside. I came out of the motel and headed to the car. I could feel a little bit of dizziness in this one as the vision seemed to jump more rapidly than the others.

"I think I know where we're going. We're very close." I put the black pick-up in drive and drove toward the highway but didn't get on. We drove east of the highway but the vision jumped into an attic of some kind. I must've been standing on some sort of pull-out steps leading to the attic. The top half of my body was inside the attic and I was looking around. Then I held a folder, the kind that held papers with a thin strap on the outside to hold it shut. I pulled out a notebook that had a lot of writing on all the pages. I wasn't reading the pages but fanned through them. As I put the notebook back in the folder, I found a piece of paper lingering by itself and it fell to the attic floor.

It stopped. My head went back to normal but I was more disoriented this time. I had to blink my eyes several times to make them focus. It seemed who or whatever was sending me messages was getting more intense. My head seemed to hurt a little more each time and visions were staggered as if they, he, she, it; whatever was in a hurry. The vision itself didn't seem intense or scary so I figured we must be getting close to some answers but obviously not in Savannah. Why did it send us here? What a huge waste of time!

"Jesse, finally! I've been calling your name and you just kept holding your head. Was it a vision? What did you see?! Are you okay?! Why aren't you answering me?" I knew she was scared, she wouldn't let me get a word in edgewise and her words were crackling as she spoke. She was kneeling in front of me grasping my wrists and she'd been crying. She shook violently.

"I'm fine Skittles. They seem to be getting more intense and I'm not sure why but I do know that we're Las Vegas bound baby."

Chapter Four

Nevada

I didn't even have to guess what vehicle the agency would give us at the airport and I didn't have to think about our next direction. We both hopped into the black pick-up and I threw the duffel bags into the king cab behind us. I followed the steps of the vision to the Motel 6 then east of the highway. I wasn't sure what to do from that point as the vision got off the highway into an attic. I hoped I'd know when we got there. I drove for a few minutes then I had a déjà vu!

"This is the street from the nightmare, first vision, whatever it's called. The first one was the scariest and an image stepped out of the mirror and handed me the envelope which held your sister's letter! It was physically in my hand when I woke up." I turned left on the street and it was exactly as I envisioned. I found the dilapidated house quickly and pulled onto the cracked driveway. I then had a horrifying thought.

"Mandy, you weren't in that one, not even in the car! I want you to stay in the truck with the doors locked. You lay on the horn if anyone approaches and I'll be out in a flash."

NO, I'm going in!" She let go of my hand and crossed her arms over her chest. I knew Mandy would be someone I would never be able to say "no" to but I had to try.

"Mandy, I don't know what we're walking into. Please listen to me and stay in the truck!"

NO Jesse. I'd be safer inside with you. I don't care that I wasn't in the first vision, I'm here now and I'm going with you!"

"Fine, you have to hold onto me the entire time and don't wander off anywhere." I wouldn't budge on that compromise.

The house and the neighborhood was exactly the same. We walked to the front door and walked into the living room. I knew in the last vision was in an attic. I looked down the hallway that held the bedroom with the mirror. Yep, not going in there. We walked down the hall toward the bedrooms and I kept Mandy's hand tight in mine. There it was, a small rope dangling from the ceiling attached to an attic door. Why didn't I notice that in the first vision?

I pulled on the handle and it released a small ladder leading to the attic. The vision wasn't real clear as to my next step but it was fairly obvious. I climbed the small ladder then looked down at Mandy who was on the first rung heading up with me.

"Please stay down there. I don't think I have to go all the way in but if I do then stay there and hold the ladder for me please."

"Fine but hurry. I'm scared and this place is really creepy."

I continued to the top and looked into the attic. It was very warm and musty smelling. There was nothing in the attic but old somewhat pink insulation still in the paper wrapping. It must've been sitting there a long time as the part that stuck out was an off pink, discolored. Someone had laid it in the attic but never got around to spreading it out. I knew at this point that I'd have to go inside.

"Mandy I will be right back I promise. I have to go in further."

"Okay but be careful."

The wood of the attic floor was rotten and made a terrible squeaking noise when I moved. I looked around and saw a small window that faced the front of the house. I walked carefully toward the window when my shoelace got hooked on a loose board. In my vision I had found a folder of some kind, maybe it was under this floorboard? The board was about 8 inches long and came off with ease. I carefully laid it to the right of me, being careful of the rusty nails sticking through.

Inside the hole I made from pulling the board up was a black vinyl folder. It was the size of a small briefcase but not as thick. It had a flap with a silver clasp that held it shut. Exactly like my vision! I opened it and inside was a hard bound three-ring notebook, about six inches thick. I opened the notebook to find papers filled with some sort of scientific formulas. I flipped through them and they all looked the same to me. I started to put the notebook back when I noticed a piece of paper by itself inside the vinyl case. It was a hand written note.

"Jesse, if you're reading this then something went very wrong. Please guard this with your life. I will be giving you further instructions with more visions. I'm so sorry to have put you through this but these papers are a matter of life and death! If they get into the wrong hands, well, I don't even want to think about what could happen. For now, go back to the Motel 6 and get a room. I know you have a zillion questions, I promise I will answer them when the time is right but for now, this is the best I can do. I will give you further instructions soon. Thank you so much."

"What could this possibly have to do with Mandy's sister? And how does this person know me?!" I whispered to myself.

"Jesse?" Mandy snapped me out of my little world and I climbed out of the attic.

"Okay, tell me what's in there? Is it about Cassie? Where is she? Jesse, talk to me." I grinned at her, took her hand and gently pulled her out of the house to the truck.

"I will if you let me get in a word." We were in the truck by then and holding hands again over the console.

"I'm sorry, go ahead." Mandy blushed and looked down at our hands.

"It's a notebook filled with papers. They're a bunch of formulas or something. There's a note but I couldn't make any sense of it. It's just more mystery and I don't know what all of this would have to do with Cassie." I pulled the note out for her to read.

"So we're supposed to go back to the motel and what, wait?" Mandy's eyes were filled with questions I couldn't answer.

"Yes, for now we go back to the motel. There's not a doubt in my mind that whoever is behind this will find a way to send us some kind of message as to the next step." I tried to make my voice soothing, comforting but her face yearned for solid answers. My next reaction even took me by surprise but I was so caught up in the moment, I didn't think. I put both of my hands tenderly on each of Mandy's cheeks, pulled her face close to mine and kissed her full lips. She didn't resist and she opened her mouth slightly and tilted her head to the right. Her breath was warm and her breathing increased as did mine. I could have stayed in this moment forever but reality hit me like a ton of bricks. I snapped out of the fairy tale realizing how forward I had just gotten.

I pulled back still holding her cheeks and waited for the slap on the face. Instead, she looked at me questionably and pulled her head back to her seat. I saw the 'want' in her eyes and couldn't believe I could be this lucky. I knew I had to do the right thing even though it was killing me. Mandy was devastated by her sister's disappearance and I refused to take advantage of her vulnerability. *There better be a Heaven, resisting this temptation should wipe out any sins I may have committed.* I thought to myself and tried hard not to smile. I didn't want to ruin the moment more than I already had.

"We better get back and see where the next part of this journey takes us." I gathered the vinyl case with its contents and took Mandy's hand. She stared at me with silent questions.

We got to the Motel 6 and got a room. Surprisingly, Mandy wanted one room for both of us and I convinced myself it was because she felt safer. I didn't want to get my hopes up that she wanted me even though the "almost kiss" might suggest that she does.

"Okay, here's your key and a map of the motel. There's an outdoor pool with a Jacuzzi, restaurant and lounge. Please enjoy your stay and let us know if you need anything." The woman smiled.

It was only 4:00 in the afternoon but we decided to head to the room and settle in before deciding our next move. The room was typical with a queen sized bed; night stands on either side; built-in dresser that the TV stood on; a big mirror above the dresser; a closet area near the bathroom on the opposite side of the vanity and it had a sliding glass door with a small balcony like the motel we stayed in last night.

We unpacked our necessities and Mandy laid out some clothes for tomorrow. She utilized a couple of hangers in the closet space and hung up a green sundress and a light sweater. She stood at the closet after hanging up her clothes staring at them. I was sitting on the bed as I had everything I needed unpacked; toothbrush, toothpaste, electric razor and deodorant. I didn't bother laying out any clothes. Instead, I watched Mandy. She never missed a beat when moving around. She flowed through her space like she was on a cloud. It fascinated me.

"Mandy, are you okay?" I loved saying her name; actually I was beginning to love everything about her. This was very strange and scary. I always had my emotions in check, I was a cop for God's sake and after losing Stephanie to my job, my walls were pretty thick. How had Mandy managed to get through at least a layer of the wall without even trying?

"What? Oh, yeah I'm fine. I was just thinking about that 'vision', episode or whatever it is you had." She walked into the room and sat on the edge of the bed next to me. I decided a fun distraction was in order and if I sat near her any longer I would probably lose control of what little restraint I had.

"How about we go down to the lounge, I think there are some slot machines there? Let's see how much money we can lose." She nodded and took my hand that I offered her.

We headed downstairs and found the lounge immediately. I ordered us a couple of beers and then gave Mandy some ones to put into the machines. She went around to the second machine that sat behind us. I sat at the one next to her. I could see her with my peripheral vision and noticed she took something out of her purse. I looked to see what she pulled out, I should've known, a bag of Skittles.

"What happens if you run out of your supply?" I started laughing.

"Hey, smarty pants you have no room to talk. I caught you red handed watching Scooby Doo." We both laughed and continued playing our machines.

The machines we played were quarter slots. After losing ten dollars in mine I moved to the machine on the other side. I hadn't sat down for 2 minutes when the bell on the top of her machine starting flashing and making a horrendous noise! Everyone in the lounge, all eight of us including the staff, came running to Mandy's side. She stood up and backed away terrified.

"Mandy, you won!" I gave her a bear hug lifting her up off the floor and swung her around without thinking of how she might feel about that. I looked at the floor and saw multi-colored Skittles all over the place. She had dropped her bag and it exploded on the floor.

"What?! I thought I broke the machine or pushed a button I wasn't supposed to." She told me after I put her back on the carpeted floor.

"Have you never gambled before or seen someone win big?"

"I gambled a couple times in Billings but never won and didn't pay attention to all the noises."

"You just won $5,000!!" The sirens and flashing finally stopped and the people standing around us congratulated Mandy. I could tell that all the attention was starting to make her uncomfortable so I took her hand and led her to the bar. I glanced at the bartender and he nodded his head while getting Mandy another beer.

"You can cash that in at the front desk. Congratulations honey. You're the first big winner in a week. What a stroke of luck!" The bartender told her when he put the beer in front of her.

"Thank you but it's not mine. Jesse it's your winnings. That was your money I put into the machine. I'm not taking it."

"Mandy, that's not how it works. It was your luck that rubbed off on those bills. It's yours Skittles! Smile, you just won big!" She finally relaxed and got excited. I just sat back and watched her, every minute with her made me feel I've known her for years.

"I won. I WON? I've never won anything in my life! Well, show trophies but that doesn't count." She turned her barstool to the side to face me, I stood on her right. Her ginger eyes glowed and the smile on her face melted me like the spring snow under the bright sun.

"Yes you did and you deserve every penny!" But the smile left her face and she got very serious.

"Wait. I'm splitting it with you, if you won't take it all then you at least have to take half of it." I could tell she meant it and tried to be firm with her statement but she was so adorable when she was being serious that I had to hold back a laugh. I knew that would upset her.

"Let's cash it in and we'll talk about it later." I had put my hands around her tiny waist and stood between her legs. She had placed her hands on my waist and our faces were inches from each other. She pushed me away a few inches.

"Scooby, there's nothing to talk about! It's only fair and if you don't take the money then I'll give your half to the staff here. I mean it!" The more she tried to be mad the more I tried not to laugh and she caught on to that. "Ugh! You are so frustrating Jesse!" Then she smiled and pulled me closer.

"I know, I've been told that by more people than I can count." We stared into each other's eyes for several moments. Mandy broke the silence and startled me with her next statement.

"Let's go upstairs." She started to pull my head to hers and when our lips almost touched, she gently pushed me backwards so she could jump off the stool. I couldn't believe my ears. Who was I to argue, I'd already frustrated her and the least I could do was what she asked this time. I tried not to get my hopes up, with my luck we'd get upstairs and she would come to her senses and start running for the hills.

Mandy held my hand all the way to the room and squeezed it several times. Luckily, she only drank the first beer so I knew it wasn't the alcohol talking. I would've found a way to persuade her to wait if she had had more to drink. Oh, who was I kidding? I'm a guy; I probably would've obliged then felt guilty in the morning. I was relieved I didn't have that worry but I was still apprehensive. I was feeling so many emotions about this wonderful lady that I didn't want her to do anything SHE might regret in the morning. I was going to have to be careful, she was fragile emotionally, and it might be a balancing act to make sure she would be okay.

I unlocked the door and she walked in front of me grabbing my hands from behind her. This moment on I was following her lead and letting her make the decisions about tonight. This could make us or break us. If we followed through then she might be so horrified at what she had allowed that we would never be the same or, and this was the one I prayed for; she would realize I was the best thing that had happened to her and have no regrets. I shook my head with those thoughts and put all of my concentration on this beauty in front of me.

She stopped at the bed still holding onto my hands but didn't turn to face me right away. *Oh, here it comes. "I'm sorry Jesse, I don't know what I was thinking and I'm not ready."* I thought to myself, almost sweating waiting for the hammer to fall. It didn't fall.

Mandy dropped my hands and turned slowly around to face me. Her face was completely serene, a want in her eyes so strong that no man alive could resist her. Our bodies stood one inch from each other. She stared up at me with those ginger colored eyes. We stood like that for several moments. I resisted the urge to grab her waist and toss her on the bed. *Let her lead Jesse, don't be a fool.* My body ached and my mind raced. I felt I would jump right out of my skin if something didn't happen soon but I stood my ground.

Finally, she put her hands around my waist and pulled me into her letting that inch of space disappear. Now our bodies touched, both heart rates accelerated and beat so hard that they cancelled each other out. I put my hands gently on her cheeks and pulled her face to mine. I kept her face just a fraction from mine, holding it and looking straight into her eyes. I could feel her breath and the longer I held her there the faster her breathing. My heart pounded and the blood rushed through my veins like it was on fire.

I was just coming in for the most passionate kiss of my life when it happened. The timing could not have been worse if it tried. My head started throbbing and my body stiffened from my neck to my knees. I couldn't move or breathe. I heard Mandy's voice but it was miles away.

"Jesse, what's wrong. Jesse talk to me, you're scaring me! Jess, please!" I could feel her trying to pull my hands from her face but I couldn't move. *Please don't let allow me to hurt her!* It was as if I had become paralyzed physically and mentally only noticing half of what my surroundings held before me. I felt my arms drop to my side and my body move to the bed. Mandy must have managed to get me that far but then she disappeared, everything disappeared. All that surrounded me was blackness and silence at first.

Then a male voice filled my head. I figured I was about to have another vision but this was more extreme than any of them. I was getting flashes in my mind but they didn't make any sense. It felt like my head was imploding again and was being downloaded. The male voice was breaking up as if the connection was bad. I couldn't understand a word, just heard a male voice. Then, as if we had come out of the hills and the landscape was flat, the connection was crystal clear and the flashes vanished, just a voice and blackness in my head. I couldn't hear or see anything in the real world.

Jess, I'm so sorry to do this to you. I never intended to burden you with any of this. I wanted to lead you the way

75

through visions that wouldn't hurt you, lead you to the final destination then leave you alone. But we're running out of time. They're about to inject me again. I don't know how long I'll be out this time and Cassie won't last much longer. They're getting impatient and have realized I won't give them what they want, they're going to kill her and it's all my fault. Once they put me 'out' then I won't be able to control my thoughts and lead you the rest of the way. I still need you to find her, Mandy's sister, Cassie. I've been able to 'see' her but I can't tell where she is. They've been sedating me just enough to mess with my powers. Find her and keep her safe until I can find a way out of this and make it back to her.

You're going to feel some strong sensations, it's not dangerous but when it's done, you will have the tools you need to find Cassie. I led you to Mandy so you could keep her safe while on your quest for Cassie. I worry that they may come after Mandy as well.

I wanted to do a partial transfer but they're not giving me enough time. I will have to transfer everything I possess. I know this is impossible to understand and I've turned your life upside down, I'm so sorry. If there was another way, I swear I would do it but there's not and I don't have time to fully explain. Please go with this, the more you relax the easier and faster the process. When the process is done do what your new found powers tell you. Your instincts will be heightened and your new powers will start to show themselves, don't be alarmed and let them do their job. I promise we will meet someday soon and all your questions will be answered.

Hold on to the papers you found today and guard them with your life. I must leave you now, God's speed and take care of our girls. Oh one more thing, Mandy feels the same way about you. Okay, the 'process' will begin in 30 seconds.

I was powerless to move, talk or even respond to him in my mind. I wanted to argue with him and tell him to go to Hell but I couldn't. I wanted to tell him that I was sick of being his puppet and watching Mandy go through all the turmoil this brought into her life. I wanted to punch him, how does one punch a voice? UGH! This was so frustrating! I promised myself that when I did meet this 'voice' I would punch his lights out then let him answer all my questions.

My eyes were open but I could not see anything except blackness and all I heard was a soft humming in my ears, no other sound. I felt Mandy's presence, but could not hear or see her. My body started convulsing. Every nerve and vein seemed to contract. The blood rushing through my veins and heart made a horrible pounding in my ears; it was so loud that my ears ached. My body felt like it had been thrown into a vice and someone was folding me in half like a twig.

I was sure Mandy could see me folding, probably see my bones start to protrude through my skin. Would she call the coroner or paramedics? Maybe the people with the strait jackets that would be the smart call to make. I couldn't talk to her, tell her I was okay and the 'voice' assured me this was safe. HA, what a joke! The 'voice' told me it wasn't dangerous but did he tell me how long I would be in the Funny Farm?

I continued to fold and twist, it was excruciating. My torso and head felt most of the pain. Then it stopped, silence; no pounding of blood in my head and ears but my body and mind were still paralyzed. I couldn't see or hear anything, total silence and blackness filled my world again.

Here it goes again, it wasn't over! Instead of twisting and folding in half this time, my body was ice; like someone had dumped me into a frozen river. My teeth chattered so loud and hard I was afraid when it was over that my tongue would be bitten in half and my teeth would be scattered all over the bed. What had I done to this man to deserve this? My limbs felt brittle and if my body convulsed any longer they would all fall off. Just kill me, kill me and get it over with.

The freezing stopped and I was afraid to move; terrified to open my eyes to see the horror in Mandy's face. Maybe she used her survival instincts and fled, that would be the safe and smart thing to do. I closed my eyes as tight as they would go, maybe if I laid here long enough without moving then it would all go away. I would wake from this nightmare. I couldn't tell what the "process"; the hell he just put me through did to me. What "Powers" did he mean?

I slowly opened my eyes and stared at the ceiling for a moment. I think I had control of my body again but I wasn't sure, I was petrified to try. I imagined my arm falling off from the shoulder when I tried to get up and maybe my head staying put on the bed as my torso rose up. Who knows what the freezing did to my limbs. If that wouldn't put Mandy over the edge then I don't know what would. Then Mandy's gentle touch on my arm startled me but I still did not move. I was afraid the convulsing or freezing would start all over again.

"Jesse, Jesse where did you go, what happened? Jesse, talk to me!" Her voice was barely a whisper. She must've been afraid that it would start all over again as well. I wondered what she had witnessed me do. There was no way for me know what my body had done with this 'process', I couldn't control anything. I had to get this over with and find out what a freak I was now. Had I changed into the Incredible Hulk or maybe a Werewolf?

"Mandy, are you okay? Did I hurt you?" I turned my head slightly to the right to see her face. She was sitting on the bed next to me. Her face was wet from tears and she was shaking. Oh God, look at what I had done! I terrified her! She still sat next to me though, how could that be? Why didn't she run screaming?

"Hurt, ME? What are you talking about?! I thought you were dying! I couldn't snap you out of it and I didn't know what to do! I wanted to call 911 but I was afraid to leave your side and find my phone. Your body was convulsing and I was scared you would bite your tongue off. I started to get up and make the call when you cried out Cassie's name."

"I did? I don't remember that. I don't remember saying anything. I couldn't even hear my own voice! I just know how I my body felt like it was being folded in half but turned to freezing. I couldn't see anything, it was black and sometimes there was roaring and pounding going on in my head. When it finally stopped I was worried that I turned into a giant monster. I was so scared that I had hurt you somehow. I couldn't open my eyes to find out what I had done while I was, wherever I was. Then I felt your touch and I can't begin to explain the relief I felt but I still didn't know if I had hurt you." I took her dainty soft

Tracy Plehn

hands into mine and held them tight trying to reassure her that everything was okay. I wasn't sure I could pull that off when I didn't know myself that everything was okay. I had no idea what had just been "transferred" into my brain.

The 'voice' told me to do what the Powers said, go with it. What in the Hell does that mean?! Right now, I feel fine. I don't feel any different than before the 'process'. I couldn't make sense of any of it.

"Well, maybe the best thing for now is to get some sleep. We'll try to figure out this whole mess in the morning." I suddenly felt exhausted and couldn't keep my eyes open.

"Okay, but are you sure you're alright? Should I find a doctor or maybe take you to the hospital?" Mandy was still shaking.

"No, I promise I'm okay. Let's get some sleep and I'll tell you everything I remember in the morning."

Mandy went into the bathroom to get ready for bed and I took off my jeans and shoes and hoped sleeping in a t-shirt and boxers wouldn't offend her. I was too tired to worry about it at length. I lay down on the bed staring up at the ceiling. My mind was racing but my eyes and body were beyond tired. Obviously, my brain would win this battle because it hit me...the 'voice' had told me to "take care of OUR girls"! What did he mean "our" girls? Could this 'voice' be from Damien?!

Mandy was still getting ready for bed and was standing in the vanity area outside the bathroom. I noticed one thing, my hearing was unbelievable. I could hear the toothpaste coming out of the tube and the bristles of her toothbrush rubbing together! *Could this be one of the 'Powers' he spoke of, bionic hearing? That's pretty cool. How many are there?*

The exhaustion I previously felt had vanished. I suddenly felt I could solve all the mysteries of the world but would have to start with my own little world. I found a pad of paper and pen in the bedside table drawer and started a journal of sorts. I wrote everything I could remember this 'voice' saying to me and the new things I noticed about myself. I would get a real journal tomorrow and document everything. For now, this pad of paper would have to suffice. I sat on the bed and wrote things down frantically when Mandy's hand on my shoulder about shot me through the roof.

"I'm sorry; I didn't mean to scare you." *I thought he was tired?*

"I was tired but I decided to map out what we're doing tomorrow before going to sleep."

"Huh? I didn't say anything about you being tired. I thought I scared you when I put my hand on your shoulder and I felt bad."

"You didn't say 'I thought he was tired'?" *Holy crap! Can I read her mind?! Had she thought that question? I heard it plain as day!*

"No, I said I was sorry if I scared you." *Maybe I did say that out loud. How would he have known what I was thinking? Impossible, I must've said that out loud. That's embarrassing.*

Oh my God, I'm looking right at her and her mouth is not moving but I can hear everything she's saying, well thinking! I can't let her know; she will be so freaked out and will be afraid to be around me. She'll be worried about everything she thinks about. There's got to be a way to turn this off, I feel like I'm invading her privacy. I am invading it! It would be cool to know how she really feels about me though. You fool! Focus, we have work to do!

"You didn't scare me. Oh, did you tell me the kind of work Damien does?" I decided changing the subject was the best thing for now.

"Some kind of scientist I think." *Where did that question come from?*

"Okay, I'll finish up here then get some sleep. I'm so sorry about all this weird stuff. I'll figure it out though. You sleep and I'll take this over to the table." *God, she's gorgeous and so sweet.* I moved off the bed and walked over to the small round table in the corner of the room. I could feel her eyes on me as I walked away and that made me feel pretty good.

He has such a nice body. How far would we have gone if this 'thing' hadn't happened to him? He felt so good and his body, holy cow! Mandy, control yourself! I tried turning off the volume or at least turn it down but I still was able to "hear" everything she thought.

She was climbing under the covers and I walked back to the bed and gave her a kiss on the forehead. I pulled the covers around her and turned off the bedside lamp. She smiled at me and I almost forgot what I was doing. Then she turned on her side and I remembered. I realized as I turned around that I had not heard a thought this time from her. Did it work, had I turned off her 'thoughts'. I tried a small experiment and turned back to face her, she was still facing the other direction. I looked at her and concentrated then her thoughts came flooding back in my head...

What's going to happen when this is all over? How do I tell a man I've known for two whole days that I've fallen in love with him? He'll go running for another country....

I shook my head and it turned off. Wow, that was easy to do. *She loves me too!! I can't believe it! She doesn't know that I just cheated and invaded her brain space. I will have to tell her how I feel soon without letting on that I can read her mind.*

I finished writing everything I could remember about the 'process' and climbed into bed next to Mandy. She was sleeping but it didn't seem a very peaceful sleep. Her eyelids fluttered rapidly. She had a tense look on her face and she was trembling. I wanted to 'tap' into her mind to see what was disturbing her but decided against it. As I settled in she must've sensed I was there because she moved in closer and put her head on my chest. I put my arms around her, the trembling stopped and she seemed to relax. It didn't take long for my own exhaustion to return and take over.

Chapter Five

The next morning I woke to find Mandy gone. Panic set in and I wasn't sure why, for all I knew she could've been in the shower. I jumped out of bed and hurried to the bathroom calling her name. No answer, she wasn't in the room. *Okay, maybe she went downstairs for coffee, relax Jesse. If I concentrate, can I hear her thoughts if she's not near me?* Okay, that didn't work because I heard nothing but my own thoughts.

"Cassie? Cassie, is that you? I haven't seen you in a long time. How have you been?"

"Huh? Who me?" Mandy took the two cups of coffee from the lady at the counter and turned to face the man that was talking to her.

"Yeah, how are you?"

"You must know my sister, her name is Cassie! Sir, please tell me the last time you saw her! She's been missing and I've frantically been trying to find her!" For the first time in weeks Mandy had an ounce of hope about her sister.

"Hmmm, it must've been last year sometime. You're her sister? Unbelievable! You must be twins?"

"Yes we are identical twins and she's been missing for several weeks." Mandy was trying to hold back tears.

"I'm so sorry. Do you think your sister's here in the area?" The man asked, stepping a little closer to Mandy.

"We don't know. We got a couple of clues that brought us here."

"We? Is your husband with you?"

"No he's not my husband, it's a long story." Mandy took a step back toward the counter as she began to feel a little uncomfortable but the man stepped even closer to her. She could smell his cologne, not sure of the brand. His hazel eyes tightened somewhat and he put his hand on Mandy's arm as he bent in to speak softly to her.

"Mandy, I need you to come with me. Don't make a sound or act differently as we have eyes on your friend and we won't hesitate to take him as well." He tightened his grip on her arm and led her toward the front door. Mandy moved quietly with the stranger still holding the two cups of coffee.

I decided it was taking Mandy a long time to get breakfast and started worrying. The pounding pain in my head began for only a few short seconds this time but what it left in its quake was worse than the physical pain I endured last night. Mandy's terrified beautiful face filled my thoughts. I concentrated as hard as I could so I could figure out if this was real time or something that was about to happen.

A black SUV with tinted windows stood in view of me, wait, it's Mandy. I'm seeing through her eyes! The vehicle is in front of her in a parking lot. Mandy, turn your head so I can see where you are and who you're with. She did it, as if she heard me! She turned her head to the left and looked right into the eyes of a man. What was he doing? He walked so close to her but then she looked down at her left arm. The man was holding her arm; he was forcing her to walk with him. I couldn't tell what he was doing with his left arm, if he had a gun to her. His arm looked to be shoved under his shirt so I was pretty sure he held a gun. Mandy's gaze turned to the right and I could see they were still in the hotel parking lot!

I rushed out of the room and through the door marked "Stairs". I skipped 2-3 stairs at a time trying to get to Mandy. I burst through the front door of the motel leading to the parking lot running through all areas of the lot. I couldn't find her. I didn't see a black SUV anywhere. I concentrated on Mandy's face and closed my eyes tight to really see her. I didn't know all of my abilities or whatever they were called and didn't know if I should try to read her mind or try to have a vision as to what would happen.

"Just think, picture her face, the man that walked next to her. Who was he, what the hell did he want with Mandy? I'll kill him if he touches a hair on her beautiful head!" I didn't know how close someone had to be in order to read their mind, what if she was miles from me now, could I find her? Then I remembered that Damien or

whoever cursed me with this was in another country for all I knew and he found me so finding Mandy should be a piece of cake.

It seemed like hours that I stood there with all these thoughts and questions but it couldn't have been more than seconds. My eyes flew open and I caught the image of the black SUV again and the man pushing Mandy through the passenger door, her face wet with tears and she was trying to scream but he had his hand on her mouth. Her thoughts were so terrified that I couldn't make them all out.

That did it, I turned to the right, not sure why but just turned. I still had the images in my head and now the man was putting a piece of duct tape on her mouth and tying her hands and feet. I couldn't run fast enough but why can't I find them? This parking lot is not that big.

If this whining bitch doesn't be quiet I'll put a bullet in her head, I don't care what the boss says. I might have some fun with her first though. I heard these disgusting thoughts of the man shoving Mandy around and I had never been more enraged in my life. I rounded the back end of the hotel and there it was, the black SUV and the vile man. Wait, there's two men. The bastard manhandling Mandy was getting in the front passenger seat and the other man was in the driver's seat. What I was seeing was real time and not visions of past or future happenings.

I didn't know how much more hard running my lungs could take but they were going to have to give more. I ran as fast as I could but the SUV had too much of a head start on me. It left two black marks on the pavement as it sped off. My only other option was to run to our vehicle before I lost their sewer filled minds. I didn't know my powers well enough to figure out from second to second which one to use, exactly what they all were, how many I had or what this all meant. I only knew that I had to find her and not let these S.O.B.'s out of my range.

It didn't take me long to reach our vehicle even though it seemed like hours. I had stashed my Glock under my seat, I didn't want Mandy to happen upon it and freak so I hid it. I yanked it out and put it in the console between the front seats, turned the key, put the truck in drive and tore out of the parking lot. At this point, all I knew is they turned left out of the lot, probably going to the highway which was about a mile up the road.

My head started to ache a little as I started hearing voices in my mind but it was all so confusing. I couldn't tell if the voices were from the pigs I was chasing or someone in another car. I figured out awhile ago that my head pounded when I was about to have a vision and it seemed now that it only ached when peoples' thoughts invaded the space between my ears. It didn't hurt, just annoying. I was disappointed to find these particular voices were those of the car that flew past me. I caught a quick glimpse and it was a young couple arguing. I had to keep going, keep trying.

"Pull into those trees over there out of sight."

"Why? We need to get her to the rendezvous point or TJ will kill us."

"PULL OVER IN THERE! We're ahead of schedule, they have the freak they're holding in the lab subdued so he can't find us and I want to have some fun before we hand her over to TJ. We can both have fun and be on our way, no one will have to know. Now pull over!"

The black SUV pulled into a group of thick trees and bushes and made its own path to the center out of sight of the road. Mandy could hear every word the men were saying and knew exactly what the SOB was talking about and what he wanted. Mandy had been trying desperately to free herself but to no avail. The ropes around her wrists were too tight and she couldn't budge. She closed her eyes so tight to concentrate that they made her cheek bones ache. She pictured Jesse's face, his strong hands and muscular body and his gentle light blue eyes. She pretended she was wrapped in his strong arms and these maniacs didn't exist.

Her thoughts were interrupted when the SUV's engine turned off and the man in the passenger seat was opening her door. He yanked at her ankles so hard that they felt they would crumble under the pressure. She slid down the seat and side of the car on her back hitting her head on the metal part of the door jamb then on the hard ground.

The revolting man grabbed the rope that bound her hands behind her back and yanked her up on her feet. Mandy tried to hold all emotion in but the tears and fear would not stay down. He drug her by her wrists a few feet from the SUV and threw her face down onto the hard dirt and pebbles. The driver of the SUV stayed in the car.

"Alrighty then, time for some fun sweetheart. You know you'll enjoy it." The pig turned Mandy over on her back with her hands still bound. He began to untie her ankles when the driver came running over.

"Come on Stan we gotta go! TJ just called and said he wants us there now! Get her back in the car and let's go!"

"We've got time for me to have a quickie, get off my back." He continued messing with the rope when his cell phone rang.

"Dammit, it's TJ. Alright get her back in the car and I'll let him know we're on our way."

The driver was much gentler and picked Mandy up under her arms letting her get to her feet slowly. He then put his right arm around her legs and picked her up. He laid her down in the back seat and got in the driver's seat waiting for Stan before putting the SUV in drive. Mandy was shaking violently and could barely breathe. The other vile pig jumped in the passenger seat slamming the car door beside him.

"Let's go." He said as he turned around to look at Mandy. The look he gave her was frightening, evil then he turned his attention to the road and didn't speak another word.

My head began to pound. I drove furiously down the stretch of road toward the highway. I wasn't sure which way to go once I got there until a thick clump of trees and bushes came rushing into my head. I pulled the car over to let the vision take over....

I could see the passenger getting out of the SUV and walking around the vehicle. He was an ugly brute with greasy thin dark brown hair that hung just below his neck line. He was only about 5'8" and must've weighed 200 lbs with a belly that protruded out over his pants. He had beady round eyes and a big nose. There was a tattoo on his left arm, I think it was a snake wrapped around some sort of stick but I couldn't be sure.

The vision turned to Mandy but she wasn't in the car. She was weeping uncontrollably on the ground and the man had his hands on her! He was untying her ankles! NO! My head was beyond pounding and I could feel the blood rush to my head and my jaw began to ache from clenching my teeth so hard.

Fortunately, the disgusting pig was interrupted before he could harm her and they were back in the SUV but where were they? Then my head stopped pounding and I could see Mandy clearly lying in the back seat. She was still bound and her mouth taped. Her beautiful eyes were terrified and red from crying. I could tell it was hard for her to breathe and her whole body was shaking. She looked at the driver of the SUV. *Keep looking at him Mandy so I can get into his brain and become his eyes.* How did I even know I could do that or talk to her with my mind?! UGH!

It worked and was as if she heard me and she scooted a little closer to the edge of the seat and pushed with her feet on the door to get a better view of his face. It was a profile image but it was more than enough for me to be where I needed to be. I looked at Mandy one more time before getting into the man's head and she looked more confused than frightened now.

I decided to take advantage and reassure her that I was with her and on my way. I was finding it easier to switch to whichever power suited me without thinking too hard about it. Skittles, *I'm on my way. Please hang in there and anything you can see out the window might help me locate you. I'm going into the driver's head now so I can see the road but I'm close.* I saw her understand and relax slightly.

I could see the scenery flying past but I had to keep switching from my head to his so I wouldn't crash into something or someone. That made it very difficult to concentrate on their location but then I saw it, a billboard they had just passed several minutes before and there it was in front of me! I was not only on the right path but immediately behind them! I stepped a little harder on the accelerator. I got back in the driver's head so I could see the speedometer. *Look down; look at the speed you're going.* He did it! *"This was kind of fun! Fun? Are you kidding? Jess, remember why you're having this fun you idiot. Good grief, there I go again, talking to myself!"*

The speed of the vehicle they were in was going 80 mph. They were obviously in a hurry but didn't want to take a chance on a highway patrolman. So, I put mine to 90 and knew I'd be up with them soon. I returned to my head and watched the road and anticipated the approach of their SUV.

Okay, when you see it, how will you handle the situation? Should I stay a safe distance behind and wait for them to reach their destination? Should I fly past them and force them off the road? Not the second. I might endanger Mandy more. So, stay behind them for now. There it was. They were about a ½ mile in front of me. I got a little closer then kept that distance; I didn't want to spook the driver.

Mandy, can you hear me? Can you speak to me this way or is it one sided? I got back into the driver's head hoping he would turn to Mandy and he did. Geeeez, this was getting too easy. Mandy was still wide-eyed and scared but she looked at the driver and it seemed like she knew I was there. *This is getting weirder by the second but I'll think about how insane I am and what meds I should be put on when this whole ordeal is over.*

The landscape in front, beside and behind all of us was well, boring; flat, dirt and a few cacti here and there. The sky was deep blue and not a cloud to be seen for miles. It was getting hotter as the day wore on and I was very glad for air conditioning. Then the passenger of their vehicle broke the silence.

"We're almost there." *When you think about this whole thing, that freak at the lab didn't realize that he was putting both sisters in danger when he summoned her to help find her twin. Now we will have both of these bitches and he can't do a thing about it. I can have some double fun.* I could hear that last part even though it was something he was thinking and I could feel my stomach tighten up and my arms tense. I knew exactly what he was thinking when he said "double fun". I couldn't wait to get my hands on this slimy pig. Then it occurred to me, he was thinking about Cassie! Those two idiots were leading me right to Cassie!

I slowed on the accelerator so they wouldn't get suspicious and keep on their current path. We drove about five more miles then I saw the brake lights on their SUV. The scenery had changed a little but not much. I started looking around to see if I could find the building they were going to but there was nothing in all directions. Where are they going? I got back in the driver's head because if they turned on the dirt road up ahead I would have to wait until they were out of sight to continue. The driver's head was a lot more pleasant to be in; he wasn't a pig like his partner.

I can't wait until we get there so I can get away from Stan, he's driving me nuts. I'll have to keep an eye on these two girls though or he'll, well, I don't even want to think about it. I know I turn down this road then what, 8 miles I think until we get to the house. TJ better be ready because I don't want Stan getting his hands on this girl.

Good job, whatever your name is. You keep them safe until I can get there. You just led me right to your destination. I had to be careful and get out of the person's head before my thoughts took over so they wouldn't 'hear' me and know I had them in my sights. I slowed down a little more until their vehicle was out of sight. I knew what road they were turning on and how far to the "house" where they must be holding Cassie. *I wonder if I can get into Cassie's head and reassure her that help's on the way.*

Cassie, can you hear me? I pictured Mandy's face since I knew they were identical twins and tried to find her that way. All of a sudden, I had to pull over. I saw a dark room, cellar maybe. Wait, wine cellar but all the shelves were empty. There was stone everywhere, the walls and the floor. I looked around; it was as if I was right there in the room. This was either the room they were going to put Mandy in or well, it had to be where Cassie was. Wait a minute; I think this was the room of my vision when I first arrived at Mandy's ranch! This must be where Cassie is.

Since this wasn't a vision then I must be in someone's head looking around. Cassie had to be here. I looked all over then walked toward a far wall that had a huge wooden door and there, there she was! She was alive; barely it looked like. Oh my God, what have they done to her?! She's bruised and it looks like she hasn't eaten. She's so pale, even in this dark room I can see that. I moved closer to her, this is really weird. Her eyes were open and slowly looking around the room. It's like I'm in two places at once.

Cassie, can you hear me? I'll be there soon to get you out of there. Mandy will be there as well. Cassie! She looked straight ahead, confused. *Cassie, it's okay. Please don't be scared.*

She somehow found some strength and sat up against the wall. She had been slumped down on the stone floor. She had to be so cold. She looked around the room and her eyes got a little wider. *Cassie, if the people keeping you captive come back, don't say anything. Do you understand?* She actually nodded her head and I knew she "heard" me. She didn't have the strength to keep herself upright and slumped back down to the floor. I knew she needed to get to the hospital as soon as possible.

I returned my concentration to the road and waited until they were out of sight before proceeding. I got to the road they turned down and headed slowly in their direction. Then it hit me, what would I do when I got there? I was one person against a questionable amount of people. Should I call the local police? Would the police believe me or think I was involved in the kidnapping? Even using my influence as a cop may not help. I knew whatever I did it would have to be quick before we lost Cassie; she wasn't going to make it much longer. What did they want with these two innocent girls? Damien had to be the key to this whole mess but what was it?

I decided to go on my own. Luckily, it was getting dark so these slime bags would have a harder time seeing me. I watched the miles on the speedometer and I was getting close to the eight mile mark; still no sign of a building or house. I drove a couple more miles then saw a hint of lights. There it was; a big two story house. Let me rephrase that, a big two story stone mansion. It really looked out of place for this area but it was beautiful. I found a cluster of large trees that looked to be about a half mile from the house and hid in there. I'd wait until I thought everyone was sleeping to go in and in the meantime, scope out the situation and see if I could tell about how many thugs there were. I'd really have to put these "powers" to work for this great escape.

I waited and "watched" through whatever head I could get into. I had a hard time finding Mandy and started getting frustrated. I would jump from head to head as they approached another of their thug friends hoping to get a glimpse of Mandy and figure out what part of the house she was in. From what I could gather, there were seven thug slime balls altogether including one female. She didn't look female at first but when I heard her speak to the thug I was inside of, it threw me. I listened intently as they tried to figure out the next move of their boss. I ended up in the head of the guy that brought Mandy here, the one that actually got that other pig away from her. For a thug, his head wasn't the worse one to be in. He actually seemed a little compassionate even though he was part of this mess.

"Mike, how long do we have to stay in this God for saken place? When is TJ going to make his move and why in Hell do we have another hostage?!" The female was obviously impatient and ready to be done with whatever job they were hired for.

"I don't know. We just have to be patient and TJ will let us know the next move. The other hostage is the twin sister and TJ's hoping that will give 'Wack Job' more incentive to release the information he wants." The man said whose head I was hiding in.

Wack job, is he talking about Damien? Who is Damien besides Cassie's boyfriend or ex or whatever?! This guy that I was hiding in must be TJ's right hand man. He seemed to be the only one that TJ was contacting and giving orders to.

I stayed in this guy's head awhile longer. I hoped that he would lead me right to Mandy. I was pretty sure I'd be able to find Cassie and I would get her after Mandy. I figured that Cassie wouldn't be able to walk and it made more sense to get her last.

He and the female had been talking in the kitchen and from what I could tell; it was on the backside of this monster of a house. He left the kitchen and walked down a long hall leading to the front of the house.

My thoughts were interrupted when I heard a noise behind the car and froze. I wished that these "powers" would allow me to become invisible but I'd have to make the best of it. I reached up and turned the dome light switch to the off position. I slowly got out of the car and left the door open so it wouldn't make a sound. It was pitch black except for the moonlight.

I crouched beside the car and slowly and quietly moved to the back of the vehicle. I stopped and stayed crouched beside the driver's side tail light and listened. A breeze came through at that moment and rustled through the trees but that was the only sound. I waited patiently then heard it again to my right which meant if someone was out there with a gun I was completely unprotected.

I moved to the back of the car and crouched on the passenger side and listened again. The noise sounded like crunching leaves or branches. I stayed there crouched until I heard it again. I peered around the back of the car and stared toward the sound. There it was again, someone or something was definitely out there and it seemed as though it was heading away from the car.

I had put my gun in my shoulder holster and put my right hand on it. Carefully, I unsnapped the flap and put my hand on the gun while walking toward the noise. I tried not to step on branches or anything that would make a sound but it was difficult when it was so dark. I was still crouching and taking baby steps when the sound happened again right in front of me! He, she or it must've turned around. I grabbed my gun and released the safety. The gun clicked as I stood up straight and aimed, ready for the attacker. Something was wrong because I know the sound was straight in front of me but nothing happened. I wondered if we both stood there with guns aimed but didn't know where to shoot. I didn't want to shoot if at all possible as that would give me away to everyone in the house.

A drop of sweat fell off my forehead. I didn't move and tried to breathe silently. All of a sudden through the brush in front of me was a pair of bright red eyes! They were round and whatever was attached to those eyes didn't move, just stared at me. We both stood our ground. I couldn't tell how big the person or creature was but the eyes seemed about 4 feet off the ground. Then as quickly as I saw the eyes, they were gone. I stood there stunned a few more moments listening and watching; nothing. I got back in the car and tried to breathe.

I had put the gun safely back in the holster before entering but double checked when I sat down in the driver's seat. I wiped the sweat from my forehead and decided to get back in the house through 'heads' again. It was still too early to enter the house since everyone was awake and most of the lights were on. I had to be patient. It was probably good that I had time since I was a little shaken by those eyes. Maybe my eyes and ears were just playing tricks on me. I decided if it was anything dangerous it would've attacked me while I was outside.

I was getting a little hungry and remembered I had a candy bar in the glove box. I reached over to grab it. *What the heck? Where's my arm?!* I looked at my legs and held out my hand, nothing there! I turned on the dome light and looked in the rear view mirror, no reflection! I was invisible!!

Wow, so far I can read minds, turn invisible which by the way, how cool is that?! I can get into peoples' heads, see what they see and speak to them with my mind; and I have visions. I think that's it well, so far. I also don't get those pounding headaches like before. The powers must be what, settling in? That sounds weird. "Actually, I did get a headache when I was 'talking' to Mandy earlier. I get pounding headaches when Damien or whoever it is contacts me." I realized I was talking to myself out loud, AGAIN!

"Focus idiot. You can play with your new 'powers' later when the girls are safe." I looked back at the house and part of it was now dark. They were finally winding down and hopefully heading off to bed. I closed my eyes and concentrated on the slime bag that tried to attack Mandy. I wanted to keep 'an eye' on him and make sure he was behaving himself. If anyone would stay around the girls, it would be this dirt bag. I found him passed out on the couch in the library, yeah like he reads! I decided to get out of his head and head out, no pun intended, into the hallway. I concentrated harder to find someone walking around. I had to find Mandy before I went into the house. The female came around the corner and I jumped into her head. She was still very frustrated and it was difficult to keep her thoughts straight while watching where she was walking. Her thoughts were scattered and intense. I really didn't like being in her head but didn't have a choice for the moment.

"That Son of a Bitch is getting on my nerves! I sure could use a drink! I'll bet that bastard drank all the booze. TJ is screwing this whole thing up. I know he doesn't want us in one place too long with these bitches. I'm sick of the whole mess and just want my fucking money and get the hell out of here!" I made the woman's thoughts trail out of my head for awhile and concentrated on 'watching' where she was going. She had a sailor's mouth and it really got irritating.

My head starting throbbing. I was worried that the woman would be able to hear the thunder in my brain. Why was it hurting? Then I knew...

"Jesse! Jesse! Where are you?! I can't hear you anymore. Did you find my sister? Jes...."

"What the hell?! Who was that? How, who is that?! I swear if one of those guys let that second bitch out of her 'cage' I'm gonna kill them!" The woman spun around looking up, straight ahead, down at the floor then forward again while running. I was dizzy from the spinning. I tried concentrating on where she ran. I don't know how these 'powers' work but the woman must've heard Mandy in my head! This was getting creepier by the second. I wanted to reassure Mandy but I had to keep quiet. The woman was obviously freaked out by the thought of Mandy running around the house. I knew she'd go to Mandy's 'cage' to check on her, perfect!

As I predicted, the woman went straight to Mandy. I tried drowning out her thoughts but it was difficult. I would rather hear Mandy's 'voice' than this vial woman. She fumbled with some keys in her pocket and she was shaking but she managed to put the key in the door. I wanted to scream out Mandy's name when I saw her but I had to choke it down. I couldn't let that woman know anyone was about to ruin their so-called kidnapping plan.

"She's in here. Hey, wake up! Did one of the guys just have you out of the room?"

"What? No." Mandy was trying to speak without the woman seeing her cry but it wasn't working.

"Go back to sleep." She slammed the door and her thoughts went back to the disgusting clutter as before. I caught one sentence that got my attention. She was going to check on Cassie and make sure the voice wasn't her. Mandy really had her confused and on her toes. Good job Mandy.

She walked quickly, almost running, down the stairs to the long hallway we had just left. From what I could tell, there were three levels to the house not including a basement or cellar. Mandy was on the third level. I knew we'd be heading to the cellar to see Cassie. Being in this woman's head really gave me the layout of the house. I hated her thoughts but she took me exactly where I needed to go.

It was extremely difficult to keep my thoughts bottled up and quiet, I really struggled with that. I couldn't let her 'hear' me.

We got to the bottom of the stairs where she pulled a chain to turn on the light. In front of us was the thick wooden door and the room, more like a tomb, that held Cassie. The woman reached up and turned the iron handle on the smaller wooden door that hid the window. She had to step on her tippy toes to look through the window while holding the bars. We looked around but didn't see Cassie. She fumbled for the keys again then stuck one in the huge keyhole. It made an eerie sound as she turned it to the left. I had to keep my eyes on those keys as well and would have to stay in this head until I could see where she would finally leave them. That would have to be the first thing I do when I physically go into the house, grab the keys.

She took hold of the long skinny door handle, Cassie moaned. At least I knew she was still alive but she had to be in bad shape. It seemed to me they should be worried about her condition, she wouldn't do them any good if she died now.

The huge door made a whining, deep squeak as she pulled it toward us. She seemed to brace herself in the event Cassie would jump her. That was a joke! The woman stepped inside the doorway and looked right, not seeing Cassie, she looked left. There she was, still slumped on the floor against the wall. Her blanket barely covered her legs and I could tell she was freezing. I wanted to jump out of this woman's head and grab Cassie but obviously that was impossible.

"Maybe I'm so tired that I'm hearing voices. Both of them are in their appropriate cages. What time is it? I guess I'll get some shut-eye and hopefully something will break tomorrow and we can get rid of these girls." The woman turned her head before going upstairs and there it was. A window I could climb through! I stayed in her head so I could find which room she slept in. She went to the second level to a bedroom at the top of the stairs. Oh brother, she's undressing, UGH! The keys, woman, where are the keys? Aw, she laid them on the dresser.

I jumped out of her head and back into mine. Whew! What a relief! I waited about 20 minutes hoping that would give the vile woman time to fall asleep. I put the gun in my shoulder holster and grabbed the keys to the car. Quietly I got out of the car and moved toward the house. I figured I had parked a good half mile from the house and knew no one could see the car behind the trees unless they were walking the grounds and stumbled on it. The trick would be getting Cassie to the car with as weak as she was.

I walked as quickly as I could to the house trying not to step on tree branches. I couldn't be 100% sure there wasn't someone guarding the grounds.

As I got closer to the house the ground was more at an incline. I stopped when I arrived at the oval driveway in front of mansion. All the lights were off and I listened. The only sound was a slight breeze making the leaves rustle. An occasional cricket would make its music. I had to figure out where the window was to the outside of the cellar. The house faced south so it had to be on the north, back side. I crept over the driveway but it was made of white gravel and made too much noise so I moved to the grass.

I decided to try the invisible trick. If there were outside security sensors hopefully I wouldn't set them off. But, if there were sensors how would I get the girls past them? I hadn't thought this plan through very well and there wasn't much time to beat myself up about that. Mandy and I would have to drag Cassie as quickly and quietly as possible and once outside we'd have to make as fast a run, or jog, as we could. I sure hope Mandy is up for this. I decided I would stay invisible and if someone spotted us, Mandy could continue and I would hang behind to take care of the threats. Well, that's as much of a plan as I could come up with.

I got to the only window that made sense. I looked at my arms and legs, it worked faster this time, and I was invisible. I touched the window very carefully and of course, it didn't budge. That would be too easy. It was an old window that swung open to the inside. The paint was chipping off the wood frame. This house definitely needed some TLC but what did I care? I had no choice but to take a huge risk and break the window. That would also tell me if there were outside sensors.

I found a medium sized rock and turned back to the window. Suddenly, the window just opened! What?! I knelt down and froze. Then the red eyes I saw in the brush earlier, they were on the inside! I stayed frozen and we both stared at each other a few moments then they disappeared. *Okay, the window's open, I can't get distracted by anything, shake it off.*

I took a minute to find the woman's head again; I had to make sure she was sleeping soundly. ICK, there she is! Her dreams are much more intense than her conscience thoughts! I quickly got out of that tangled mess of nightmares and back to me. I focused on the window. It looked just big enough for me to slide through. I stuck my head in first to see what I would be landing on and how far the floor was. *Good, nothing down there.* I held onto to the top of the pane and slid my legs in first with the rest of my body following. I hit the concrete with my feet. I stayed very still for a few seconds. The house remained quiet.

Sweat dripped into my eye from my forehead causing me to jump slightly. I wiped it off, still not seeing my hand. I looked to my left and saw the door of the cellar. I so badly wanted to check on Cassie but decided to proceed. I knew I would have to move very slowly as this is an old house and would probably creak with every step. Yep, I put my foot on the first step and it complained to me. Every other step made the same noise and I tried different locations on the steps but it didn't help.

I got to the top of the stairs and looked both ways down the long, dark hallway. The door to the basement was right in the middle of the hallway and I remembered the woman turned left. I proceeded in the same direction walking very carefully on the squeaky floor. I wasn't sure where the male thugs were hibernating so I had to be very silent. Four steps in the direction to the next set of stairs was an arched doorway on the right. It looked to be a den or bonus room. I had seen it briefly when I was in the woman's head. She had glanced in that direction. I peered around the doorway to make sure no one was sleeping in there. A huge brick fireplace took up the far wall and it looked to be Early 19th Century furniture scattered throughout the room. *You're such a dork for knowing what century the furniture is.*

105

Secure in the fact that no one slept in that room, I continued toward the stairs. I knew the sleaze bag that tried to attack Mandy was still in the library sleeping. I had quickly jumped into his head before getting out of the car. I at least knew where two of the thugs slept. The others must be in the other bedrooms.

As I suspected, the stairs leading up also creaked. With each step, I stopped and listened. I could hear my heart hammering and feel it racing. It sounded so loud to me that I was afraid the whole house could hear it.

Halfway up the stairs my head throbbed. I grabbed the handrail and assumed it was Mandy trying to reach me or maybe a vision was about to interrupt my rescue attempt. Extremely bad timing! But it wasn't Mandy; it was that male voice again. I hadn't heard that sound since 'it' gave me the curse.

"JESSE, JESSE!"

"Quit yelling at me, I'm right here!" I replied to the annoyance.

"I can't see you, where are you? Where are the girls? Are they safe?" He sounded hoarse, like he had a bad cold. I thought it served him right if he were sick, he deserved it for putting me through this nightmare.

"You need to leave for awhile. I'm trying to get the girls now and it's a really bad time. If I make one mistake or one little noise, I wake the thugs that are holding them."

"I don't know how long I'll be conscious, the drugs wore off but I'm not sure how long I'll be awake. Try to contact me as soon as you're all safe. Call their parents after you

get to the hospital, wait for them then hopefully I'll be able to lead you to me next."

"Okay, get out of my head! Oh when this is all over, you can be sure you and I will have words, lots of words!" I heard him laugh before leaving my head. Now I had to re-focus and continue upstairs.

I got to the woman's room and luckily her door was open. I looked down at my body to make sure I was still invisible, I had no idea how long it would last. I crept into the doorway and let my eyes adjust to the different type of darkness. Her curtains were open and the moon shone right through them, what luck. I took another step and the floor board creaked. I stopped and once again, my heart tried to jump out of my chest. She made a squeaking noise with her throat but didn't move. I tiptoed further and went for the keys. I tried to remember which boards were noisy and tried to avoid them as I moved around the room. There they were, on top of the Mahogany dresser. I could see the skeleton key to the cellar and would have to figure out which one went to Mandy's door; there were at least ten keys on the ring.

I started back to the door and thought I was home free with no creaks until I hit the one at the doorway.

"Who's there?!"

I froze. *Damn I was almost out. Invisibility don't fail me now.* How could she not hear my heart pounding? Maybe she did but I didn't dare move or turn around. Hopefully she'd see no one and go back to sleep. I heard her rustling with the covers on her bed and thought she might be getting up. That would be my luck.

"I must've been dreaming." I still didn't turn or move to see what she was doing. I stood there frozen for what seemed hours and finally she started that squeaking noise and a slight snore. Whew!

The stairs to the third level were to the right so I ever so quietly headed in that direction. I couldn't remember if the woman passed other rooms when I was in her head earlier. I hoped the other bedrooms were in the opposite direction. I stopped just at the bottom of the stairs and tried to contact Mandy. I decided I better forewarn her so she wouldn't make any noise when I came in.

"Mandy, can you hear me? Mandy, wake up it's Jesse." I waited before thinking again and I was just about to call for her again when she spoke.

"I hear you! Jesse are you okay? Where are you? Do they have you also?" I could tell she was crying.

"I'm okay. They don't have me but I'm at the bottom of your stairs. I need you to listen very carefully."

"I'm listening."

"I'm going to open the door in just a minute but you won't see me. That voice gave all kinds of weird abilities or powers, whatever you want to call them. Right now I'm invisible and hopefully I'll stay that way until we all get out of here. I need you to be ready and I will touch your hand when I get in. You need to walk very slowly, these floor boards squeak and we don't want to wake the jerks that are holding you. Does this make sense?"

"Yes, weird but makes sense. Do you know if Cassie's okay?"

"Yes, she's weak but alive. We'll get her next."

"Alright, I'm standing close to the door but out of the way. I'm ready."

This was it, no turning back. I hadn't thought of those red eyes that had opened the window until now. I felt a strong sensation that something or someone was watching me. I didn't think it was one of the thugs, it felt different than that. I shook it off and continued. I quietly went up the stairs. The stairwell was thinner than the other and much darker. I wondered if by touching Mandy it would make her invisible as well. Could I be that lucky? Yeah, right. I got the keys out of my pocket and tried each one. I knew the only one that wouldn't work would be the skeleton key. I finally found the correct one and turned it until I heard the lock click. I could hear Mandy breathing hard and had to try to calm her.

"Mandy, I'm right outside the door about to open it but I need you to calm down before we start downstairs. They will be able to hear your breathing." I had my hand on the door handle but didn't turn it until I had confirmation from Mandy.

"I'm trying to be calm. I'm scared Jesse."

"I know Skittles but I'll be right by your side and I won't let anything happen to you. I'm opening the door." Luckily it was a quiet door and I opened it just enough to walk through. There she was, the most beautiful girl I've ever laid my eyes on. I missed that vision.

"Here's my hand, can you feel it?"

"Yes, you lead the way." Her breathing had slowed somewhat but she was trembling. We stepped out of the prison they held her in and she yanked her hand back.

"Mandy, what's wrong?"

"I couldn't see my hand or arm when you touched it!"

"That's perfect! I can make you invisible! I didn't even notice but that will make this break out much easier and safer. Hopefully the same thing will happen with Cassie. It's okay, take my hand again and keep your breathing down." She took my hand but she trembled harder than before. I had to ignore it for now and start down the stairs. Mandy did really well and followed in my exact footsteps. We only hit one squeaky step but still had all the floorboards to contend with.

We made it safely to the bottom of the next flight of stairs and turned toward the hallway. I froze again when I saw a light go on in the kitchen! Damn, someone was up! It's 2:00 am, what are they doing? We both stood still again and listened. We hugged the wall in case the person came our way.

"I don't care, I want this to end now or I'm going to do whatever I want with these females!" There was a pause and then...

"Yeah, whatever, go to hell!" He must've been on the phone.

Mandy started shaking uncontrollably, we both recognized that repulsive voice. That meant at least two of the thugs were getting very impatient which made them more dangerous. The pig rummaged around in the kitchen, probably getting a snack. I didn't want to try and imagine what he looked like when he ate. The noises in the kitchen stopped and it became silent for a few minutes.

"Mandy, stay very still. He can't see us and he has to pass us to get back to the library where he was sleeping." Her breathing had turned to a wheezing noise and I knew if he passed us now he'd hear her. I squeezed her hand hoping to reassure her. I was scared she would hyperventilate. She had to calm down.

"Jesse I'm trying but he's the one that tried to....just talk to me, I need to hear your voice, well thoughts."

"When we get out of here we're going on a date so I want you to think of where you want to go. We are going wherever you want. A beach in the Caribbean; a cruise; or dinner and a movie. Whatever you want. What do you picture us doing?"

"I picture a meadow in the mountains and we get there by horseback where we have a nice picnic with no danger."

"Then that's what we'll do. You pick the mountain and I'll do the rest." The moment didn't last long when I saw his shadow move toward the kitchen doorway. The light went off and I braced myself and squeezed Mandy's hand tighter. He came down the hallway right at us! I had Mandy's hand with my left hand and my right rested on the gun attached to my left shoulder. I gripped the handle in preparation to use it. I had unsnapped the holster prior to him leaving the kitchen. I knew if the 'invisibility' failed now I would have no choice but to use my weapon. So far, so good. We stayed invisible as he approached and his smell made me nauseous and made Mandy start breathing hard again. I kept squeezing her hand which

helped a little. He had gotten a couple feet away from us when he stopped. I stopped breathing.

"Who's there?" He turned and looked right at us! He stared for a few seconds then kept going.

"I must be losing my mind. It's got to be from lack of sleep." He kept walking but we waited awhile longer to make sure he wouldn't come back.

"I think he's gone Mandy. You did really well." She was shaking so hard that she couldn't respond so I pulled her forward. We had to hurry and get out of here before she had a nervous breakdown.

We got to the door that led to the cellar which meant we were halfway to safety. I led Mandy down the stairs to the cellar door.

"Is my sister down here?"

"Yes, but she's not in good shape, I just want to warn you. I think she'll be alright when we get her to a hospital. We're almost home free." I put the key into the lock and turned. The lock made a clicking sound and without hesitating I turned the big door handle. I knew exactly where Cassie was lying. Mandy gasped and let go of my hand running to her sister.

"Mandy, we still have to be very careful and quiet." I whispered to her.

"I know but I couldn't help it, I'm sorry. She looks awful; we have to get her to the hospital!"

"I know, but first we have to get the window ready. I spotted some crates that I'll push under the window for us to climb up. I'll be right back, you stay here with Cassie." I quietly but quickly went to the two crates I saw and checked them for stability. I pushed both of them under the window for a make shift ladder.

"Okay they're ready. You go through the window first, I'll lift Cassie up and you pull her through."

"Got it. Let's go." We lifted Cassie up, each of us taking an arm; she felt like a rag doll. I reached around with my right hand to feel her pulse on her neck. It was there but very weak. We had to hurry. I had scoped out the map and called Information for the nearest hospital while I was waiting in the car. I knew exactly where to go. Once we were in the car and on our way to the hospital I would call the local police. I knew all hell would break loose once the thugs realized the girls were gone. Word would get back to whoever was holding the male voice captive but I couldn't worry about that now.

I got situated in the right place then took hold of Cassie so Mandy could climb up on the crate. She was very agile and pulled herself up and out the window. I was impressed.

"Okay, smart alec, have you done this before?"

"Ha Ha. It's amazing what being terrified will do. I'm ready for my sister." Mandy leaned into the window from the outside and waited for me to pull her up on the crate. It's a good thing these girls are so skinny, made my job a little easier. It was a challenge pulling her up there without hurting her but I managed somehow. I braced Cassie against me as I handed her arms to Mandy. We both knew that Cassie would get a little scuffed up going through the window but it would be better than the alternative. Mandy grabbed Cassie's wrists and pulled gently while I pushed from the other end. We got Cassie through without too much damage. We're almost there, I couldn't believe it! This nightmare was almost over.

I picked Cassie up and cradled her in my arms. I told Mandy to hold my arm for the invisibility experiment. It worked, all three of us became invisible. We walked quickly in the direction of the car. I tried to get into the smelly thug's head while we walked to the car to make sure he was still sleeping but I couldn't find him. I guessed there was too much distraction for me to locate him. I decided to concentrate on the task at hand, get to the car as fast as possible.

The car was just feet away from us, that half mile went quickly.

"Mandy, when we get to the car I'll lay Cassie in the backseat. When we're on the road you call the police and tell them they need to get to the house asap." I was out of breath but managed those words.

"Okay. I can't believe this is almost over and I have my sister back!" Mandy was also out of breath as we reached the car. She opened the back passenger door so I could lay Cassie on the seat. She wanted to sit with Cassie in the backseat so she crawled in first and pulled Cassie by the shoulders into the car. I took a second to look at Mandy. She cradled Cassie's head in her lap and ran her fingers through her hair trying to comfort her sister. Cassie remained unconscious.

I snapped out of it and hurried to the driver's side, hopped in and put the key in the ignition. The engine turned over and came to life. As I put the car in gear I handed the phone to Mandy to call the police. She didn't hesitate and dialed 911. She had the phone on speaker and just as the dispatch answered headlights appeared behind us! Mandy must've just noticed the lights as well, I could hear the panic in her breathing again.

"911, what is your emergency?" A raspy male voice said.

"My sister and I were kidnapped! We escaped but now they're after us again. We're going to....Jesse, what hospital?!" I yelled the hospital name and the dispatcher heard me.

"Okay ma'am, stay on the line. I'm dispatching a unit to the hospital right now. What is your location right now?"

"Jesse, where are we?"

"Sir, we're about 20 minutes out. I think I can hold these thugs off of us until we get there. I'm sure once we reach civilization they'll back off but someone needs to get to the house where they were being held. I'm sure the car behind us has already alerted the rest of the kidnappers. As far as I know, there were seven. One female and six males." I gave Dispatch the location of the house and he said he would send units to that location immediately and to the hospital. I had explained that I was a cop and gave him my badge number so he wouldn't think this was a hoax. I told Dispatch that we were okay for now and going to hang up. The voice on the other end agreed and said he would make the appropriate calls. I'm sure we had made his night.

The lights behind us gained momentum and got closer. I knew if I could hold them back a couple more minutes than they would have to back off. Their car must've gotten some sort of super power all of a sudden because they were right behind us, maybe one car length. I pressed harder on the accelerator but being on a dirt road was as dangerous as ice. I couldn't risk losing control and being at their mercy or worse, getting all of us killed in a roll over.

The road was a single car so they couldn't pass without ending up in a ditch so I just had to keep it straight and steady. Lights of the city loomed ahead and I knew it wouldn't be long but we had about a mile and a half before we hit civilization and the car behind would try to get alongside of us and force us off the road. I pressed the accelerator a bit more and the headlights behind us got a little further away.

I had no idea how long it would take the local authorities to reach the area but my only goal right now was getting to the hospital. I looked in the rearview and realized the car had turned around!

"They're panicking and heading back to regroup. I'm sure they've figured out that we called the cops. Mandy, I think we're on the downhill side of this nightmare." I put my right hand around the back of the seat and Mandy grabbed it. She squeezed it to acknowledge what I said. I had slowed to a safe speed but still going faster than the speed limit. We reached the city limits and fortunately, I had studied the map intensely and knew each street to turn on for the hospital.

Chapter Six

I pulled the car swiftly in front of the Emergency doors. Throwing the car into park I got out and opened Mandy's side door. Dispatch had called the hospital so they would be ready for us. A doctor and two interns came rushing around to our side of the car with a gurney. Mandy stayed by Cassie's side until the doctors told us both to go to the waiting area.

"They'll come get us as soon as they assess Cassie but right now we'll be in the way." I put my arm around Mandy's waist and guided her to the waiting room. I had seen it as we flew past with Cassie.

We sat in the "wanna be" leather seats that were all attached. It reminded me of airport seats except the airport didn't smell of disinfectant. We both sat down but Mandy seemed ready to spring up at any second. I knew she wouldn't relax until they got Cassie into a room she could stay in with her. Mandy leaned forward in the seat bouncing her right foot. I put my arm around her shoulder trying to calm her again. I figured it was futile but I wanted to try. She grabbed my other hand and squeezed while still bouncing her foot.

"Are you Cassie's sister?" The doctor was tall and slender and seemed to have some experience under his belt, that was a relief.

"Yes I am! Is she going to be okay?"

"She is going to be fine but she sure went through something terrible. She's badly dehydrated and malnourished. Her ribs are horribly bruised and she has cuts and abrasions on most of her body. Luckily, she doesn't seem to have any internal bleeding but we'll need to monitor her for a few days to make sure. She's still unconscious but her body will need to heal without stress and it instinctively knows how to do that. She'll probably be out for a day or so. Police Dispatch filled us in briefly. I'm sure the police will be here soon to get your statements but Cassie won't be able to tell her side for at least a day. I'd really like to check you guys out as well and make sure there's nothing to worry about." The doctor was genuinely nice and sincere, not someone going through the motions.

"No, I'm okay. I just want to be with my sister." Mandy was holding the tears at bay but I knew she wouldn't win for long.

"Well, we also need to check you out for the police reports. It won't take long then you need to get some food and rest. Cassie won't be able to have visitors for awhile and she'll need you strong when she wakes up."

"Thank you, Doctor." I shook his hand and helped Mandy out of the chair. She reluctantly agreed and knew she had been out numbered on this one. The doctor examined Mandy in another room and I waited impatiently outside the door. She came out a few minutes later.

We found the cafeteria and I had Mandy sit down at a booth while I got us some food. It was the middle of the night but I was starving. I stood at the counter not really thinking about food but about Mandy. I kept one eye on her and the other waiting for the guy behind the counter. I was not taking any chances that someone would come up to Mandy and take her again, I wouldn't be able to handle that.

"Oh crap! My head, now who's trying to get in?!" I rubbed my temples hoping that would alleviate some of the pain but it never seemed to help. Nothing would work until my head was clear of whoever was trying to invade. *As if I really needed to guess who it was.*

"JESSE! JESSE! Can you hear me!"

"I told you, QUIT yelling at me! I know this has to be Damien and I know you're worried but you are really getting on my nerves! The girls are fine, we're all at the hospital and they're monitoring Cassie. The police should be at the mansion by now and someone heading over here to take our statements. I'm going to ask them to put a guard at Cassie's door. I'm sure they won't have a problem with that."

"Thank God everyone is okay. I've been so worried! I'm sorry I yelled at you, I didn't mean to but these drugs they have me on distorts my whole thinking and to me I

sound quiet, almost whispering. Damn, someone's talking to you, I'll talk to you in a minute."

"Sir, excuse me. Are you ready to order?" It was a young guy, maybe 19 or 20 trying to get my attention about food.

"Wow, I'm sorry. I guess it's been a longer day than I realized. Yes, I'll take two Chef Salads and a basket of bread with two Cokes."

The guy put the food and drinks on a tray with two sides of dressing. I handed the money to him then put $3.00 in the tip jar. I put the tray on the table while looking at Mandy. She had put her head on the table and she was out! I sat down slowly, I didn't want to shake the booth and wake her up. I ate my food and downed my Coke then asked the guy behind the counter for a to-go container for her food.

I took this opportunity to talk to Damien and find out what to do from here and why in hell these people are kidnapping right and left. It also occurred to me that this vocabulary of powers, telepathy, and whatever bizarre adjective I could think of was becoming normal! That scared the crap out of me.

"Hey Damien. Helloooo DAMIEN! Are you there? Oh good grief, what am I doing? I'm talking to myself in my head, that's just great. Fine then, I'm going to get some shut eye, hopefully the cafeteria won't mind us crashing on their tables."

"Jesse, I'm here. Don't go to sleep yet. I need to give you whatever information I can before they inject me again. Are you there?"

"Yes, as weird as all of this is, I'm here. Tell me exactly how you're able to turn my life upside down. And why does my head hurt so bad when you or someone is trying to contact me?"

"I'll explain everything later but right now I'm going to send you a, well for lack of better words, a picture of where they're holding me. I know it's a warehouse or maybe an airplane hangar somewhere in southern Nevada. Here's the tricky part, in order to make it easier for you I will have to send you an image of my face. It will lead you right to me.

"I must not be far from you, we're in Nevada. Wait, why will it be tricky to see your face? Are you that ugly?" Damien didn't laugh but I thought it was funny.

"What a comedian. I will send you that image last because it will confuse you and be disturbing but I can't explain right now, there's no time. Is there anyone around that will distract you while this is 'downloading'?"

"Nope, just me, Mandy and the poor guy behind the counter."

"Okay, it won't take long. When my image comes up, please stay calm and go with it. All of your questions will be answered when we're all safe."

"You're starting to freak me out again." He didn't comment back. My head pounded harder and everything went black. Here we go again. This time I relaxed more and let it happen, I knew I had no choice.

Images began racing around in the blackness of my head and I felt like someone was holding down the fast forward button and put it on lightening speed...

An image of a big warehouse, the inside of it, slowed to a stop. It wasn't a warehouse, it must be an airplane hangar or used to be. I didn't see any planes and it looked really run-down. Looking up I could tell that the building was metal, rusty and the image must be inside the front door looking in. To my right was a bunch of junk; old scrap metal, rusted out tools; beer and pop cans and torn up tarps. On the back wall were some dilapidated shelves that were mostly falling off the wall. To the left was a door. The image started moving again and put me on the other side of that door in a room that didn't fit the hangar. It looked updated and more like a hospital room. The right side had a Formica counter and cupboards that took up the entire wall. There was a sink with hospital looking supplies; cotton balls, disinfectant, syringes, hand soap and rubber gloves. On the back wall was a cooler of some sort with glass doors. I could see vials of drugs or medicine, not sure which or maybe both.

The image moved again to a bed, hospital bed with an IV stand and something dripping through the IV tube. I could see a body in the bed but not a face. Could this be Damien? It had to be. Come on, show me your face and let's get this over with. I realized then to be careful what you wish for. The body sat straight up, eyes wide and looked right at me! It couldn't be Damien because it was, it was ME! What the...?! The image became distorted and started swirling in my head as if it were being sucked down a drain. What's going on? Damien come back and explain, I didn't see Your face! There was blackness again. The pounding and pain in my head disappeared.

"Excuse me, Mr. Reynolds? We were hoping to get statements from you and Ms. Tagama." Damien must have known someone was here but how? It was a local police officer, young and probably a rookie. Poor sap. If this case becomes high profile, which it probably will since kidnapping was involved, he better get every detail correct. This could make or break his career.

"Um, sure but can we let Mandy sleep a little longer? She's exhausted." I whispered to the officer.

"No problem. Let's go over to this other table." We walked to a standalone table in the middle of the dining room. The officer informed me that the house was empty when they got there. The suspects must've had an escape plan and used it very well. The house of course, is being checked from top to bottom for clues and the FBI would be involved soon.

I reluctantly woke Mandy up and explained the situation. The officer reassured her that a guard would be at Cassie's door at all times. She gave the young officer her statement. He gave us his business card and told us he would be in touch soon and to call anytime if we had any questions.

We were not out of the woods by a long shot. I knew Mandy would not leave until Cassie was released, I didn't blame her but I needed to move quickly if there was any hope of saving Damien.

It was 4 am and I didn't think the nurses would let us into her room. Luckily, the night duty nurse was sympathetic and let Mandy have a few minutes with her sister. When she came out she was crying and I couldn't tell what kind of tears streamed down that gorgeous face.

"What's the matter? Mandy what it is it? Is she..."

"She won't open her eyes! Jesse, is she going to be okay?" Mandy fell into my arms and burst into tears.

"Of course she's going to be alright. She had Batman and Robinette to save her." Mandy laughed and hugged me tighter. Then she pulled away slightly and looked up at me with those beautiful ginger eyes.

"Robinette?"

"Well, that was a delayed reaction. Yes, Robinette. You're definitely not a male but you're my Robin. It's the middle of the night and that's the best I could come up with, cut me some slack would ya?" I gently put my hand on the back of her head and pulled it to my chest. She laughed but then her body went limp. She went into a deep oblivion and I kept as still as I could so she could sleep.

Shortly after Mandy fell asleep a nurse came over.

"I'm not supposed to do this but I got approval from the doctor and we want you two to get some rest in the room adjoining Cassie's. She will need both of you strong and rested. By the way, do the sisters have any family we should contact?" The nurse was a little pudgy, about 5'2" and reminded of my aunt. She was very bubbly and helpful.

"I called her parents in Florida and they should be here later today."

I carefully got up and carried Mandy into the room the nurse reserved for us. I laid her down on the bed and put the covers over her. I decided to take the chair next to the bed. It didn't take long for me to fall asleep but it didn't seem to last long.

"Jesse! JESSE! Where are you?!" Mandy had sat straight up in bed. Her eyes were wild and she looked straight at me but didn't see me. I rushed to her bed and took her hand.

"Skittles, it's okay. I'm right here." I knew it was dangerous to wake someone in that state of sleep but I had no choice, she obviously had a nightmare. She shook violently before coming out of it. She looked at me again with calmer eyes then pulled me close. I climbed onto the bed next to her and she immediately calmed down and put her head on my chest.

"I couldn't find you Jesse. I looked everywhere but you were gone. It was so real. We were on a beach looking at the ocean on a blanket. We had a picnic and champagne. You had your arm around my shoulders and the sun was just setting over the sea. I felt so, so safe and content. Then I looked over and you were gone!" I couldn't see her face while she told me of the dream but I knew she was crying.

"Hey, would Batman ever leave his partner?! I'm not going anywhere. I'm afraid you're stuck with me until you boot me out." I squeezed her a little tighter hoping that would calm her more.

"You promise? You promise you're not going anywhere?"

"I promise. I don't know what happened but from the second I looked into your ginger eyes I knew that was it for me. Mandy you're in the depths of my soul, there is no turning back. I love you with every fiber of my being." At that moment I realized I had said the "L" word for the first time.

"Jesse, I love you too. You promise me again that you're not going to disappear? Promise me!"

"I promise. Please don't worry and get some rest." I knew I would have to break that promise for a short time while rescuing Damien. I knew it would be dangerous and Mandy had been through enough, I just hoped she would understand and forgive me.

I closed my eyes and started to relax when I heard voices, not people speaking out loud but peoples' minds.

"I'm not even going to bother giving them an update when nothing has changed with Cassie. They look so peaceful, finally." The pudgy nurse thought.

"Is this shift ever going to end? I am so ready to go home. I hope John let the dog out last night, he always forgets." Another nurse that had just walked to the nurses' desk thought. I shook my head to tune them out. I must've fallen right to sleep as I didn't remember any other voices or interruptions.

Later that morning I woke up with a jerk then remembered that Mandy was in my arms so I tried to get up without waking her. She looked content and calm, I wasn't going to interrupt that. I looked at my watch, 11:30! Wow, I couldn't believe I slept so long. I stretched and walked out of the room to see if anyone heard any news about the kidnappers. I spoke to the officer they had at the door and he told me they hadn't found them yet but the FBI and the entire local force was out looking. I knew they were long gone and stashed somewhere to regroup.

"I need some caffeine." I thought quietly to myself. I gently moved Mandy's head to the pillow and got out of the bed.

I took the stairs instead of the elevator to the cafeteria, I wanted to stretch my legs. I stood in line for some coffee and a donut. I sat at one of the tables to strategize. I knew they wouldn't let Cassie go for awhile since she had sustained so many injuries from those slime balls.

There it goes again. The pain in my head was excruciating and I knew Damien or someone was coming in.

"Jesse, it's Damien. How's Cassie and Mandy?"

"They're both fine. Cassie will recover completely but she's banged up pretty good. Oh, you never showed me your face! I only saw mine. How will seeing your face and that airplane hangar help me find you?"

"Jesse, you have to trust me, I haven't steered you wrong yet have I? Just keep the images in your head when you start the trip and they will lead you straight to me. By the way, I did show you my face. Stay with the girls until their parents get there then head out. You stirred things up quite a bit and I can tell they're panicking which means..."

"They're more dangerous, I know. Are they all out there now? The police couldn't find them at the house out here."

"Yeah, I did notice there are more of them now. They arrived early this morning and they are more vile than the ones holding me. I don't know understand why they haven't drugged me again. Wait a minute. That's it. They're setting a trap and expecting us to do exactly what we're planning only they hope the girls will be with you! That's why they're leaving me coherent so I'll contact you and lead you straight to me! Jesse, absolutely make sure Mandy stays put at the hospital with her family. She'll be safe there. Like I said, as

soon as you can sneak away, start heading in this direction and I promise my exact location will come to you. It's not a long drive from where you are so hopefully I'll see you tonight or tomorrow. Stay safe and I'll meet you soon br.... Jesse." I wasn't sure what he was going to say before my name but decided not to worry about it now.

"Okay I'll see you soon. Wait! Damien! I swear I didn't see YOUR face, only my ugly mug! What am I suppose to picture in my head? Damien! Dang it, he's gone."

I went back to Mandy's room to check on her and she was passed out. Then I went to Cassie's room. She looked peaceful, safe. Then another weird thing happened, as if I needed any other bizarre event. I was thinking how peaceful she looked but Cassie must've heard me even under all the drugs she was on.

"What? Who's there?! Help me, please!" Her face tensed up and I realized Cassie thought she was still being held captive.

"Cassie, it's okay you're safe. You're in a hospital and your sister is right next door. Your parents on their way from Florida."

"Who are you? I can't see you but I hear you. Wait a minute, am I talking to you in my mind? What, how, what the hell is going on?!" She became very agitated and the monitors began speaking a little louder. I knew I had to explain quickly and calm her down. I explained who I was and everything that had happened to get her to safety. I gave her a brief description of my "abilities". She seemed to calm a little.

"You say Damien 'gave' you these abilities? I didn't know he could do that."

"You knew of his abilities?"

"Yes, I was just learning of them when he got really weird and kind of scary. His mood was erratic which wasn't like him. He was usually very even tempered. We met at the casino in Vegas I worked at. He had returned from a long bout in the jungle, I think he had been there a year or so. We were together for a year when all of this bizarre stuff started happening. He was getting paranoid saying someone found him out, his research and worried they would be after him. I couldn't get him to calm down and finally kicked him out. I regretted it later but it was too late. When I realized people were after me I tried locating Damien but no luck." She explained that she fled. She wrote a letter to Damien and sent it to the only address she knew of hoping he had gone back. She didn't know what else to do and couldn't contact the authorities, what would she tell them?

I told her how I somehow got the letter and that's how my involvement began. I told her it took me awhile to figure out it was Damien that had been "contacting" me but we had been in contact off and on and he seemed fine, worried about the girls. I could tell Cassie still loved him and I assured her I would do everything in my power to bring him home safely.

"Jesse, you need to leave as soon as possible and save Damien. Please Jesse, I can't lose him again." I told her my plan and would leave as soon as their parents arrived and I knew the two of them would be safe.

"Jesse!" It was Mandy in the next room. She must've woken up and saw I wasn't there, that was the last thing I wanted to happen.

"I'm right here Skittles. I'm coming." I ran to her room.

"Good morning Baby. Are you hungry?" She shook her head.

"How's Cassie? I want to see her." She got out of bed and was a little light headed. I braced her against my side and helped her to Cassie's room. She sat in the chair and scooted it closer to Cassie's bed.

"I called your parents and they should be here this afternoon. Mandy, after your parents arrive I'm going to get Damien and bring him back. I didn't feel right leaving the two of you but now that your parents are coming I know you two will be fine. The guards will be at Cassie's door so you'll be protected. I'll be back in a couple of days, I promise." I knew she'd be upset but nothing like I encountered.

"NO! You are not leaving without me! I am going with you! You have to promise you won't leave without me!!" She was starting to tremble again so I told her I'd talk to the doctor and see if she could travel to calm her down. Of course, I had no intention of dragging her into the depths of hell Damien and I would be involved in. I would find a way to slip away in a few hours and just hoped Mandy would forgive me. If she didn't, at least she would be alive so I could live with that. The thugs thought we were all heading in Damien's direction so they would have all their forces out there, the girls would be safe.

I sat with the girls until their parents arrived. We all introduced ourselves and I told them I wish I could've met them under better circumstances. As Mandy and their mom were catching up I pulled their father aside and explained my plan. I told him how adamant Mandy was about coming with me and he agreed that she did not need to tag along. He assured me that both of them would stay with their daughters until I returned. We exchanged cell phone numbers so we could keep in touch while I was away. As I reached out to shake his hand he surprised me by giving me a hug.

"Jesse, I owe my life to you for saving my babies. I don't know how Mandy met you and I'm sure we'll hear the whole story soon enough but I am so glad she did find you. Thank you from the bottom of my heart." He began to tear up.

"Mr. Tagama I'm the one who is grateful. I've only known Mandy a short time but I know that she is my other half and I am so grateful to have found her. You don't have to thank me because I would give my life for her. She may never forgive me for leaving but she'll be safe." We both went back into Cassie's room and they were still talking up a storm. Their mom noticed I walked in and rushed over to give me hug. She was crying so hard that words would barely come out.

"Mr. Reynolds, thank you so much for saving our girls! You are an angel and we will never forget what you've done for our family!" She took my hands into hers and put them up to her cheek. Her tears ran through my fingers.

"Jesse?" Mandy had been watching as her mother sobbed and hugged me. I walked to her bed and sat down next to her.

"I feel much better and now that mom and dad are here to be with Cassie, you and I can get Damien." Her father heard Mandy and came to my rescue.

"Mandy, you're not going anywhere sweetheart until I buy you lunch and we catch up on things. I think Jesse needs to check in with the authorities and find out the latest, right Jesse."

"Absolutely, you read my mind sir. Mandy, you spend time with your family and I'll see you soon. I love you." Leaving her was going to be the hardest thing I've ever done but I knew it was the only way to keep her safe. I gave Mandy a hug and kiss then walked out with their parents.

"Mr. Tagama, thank you for covering." I looked into those brown eyes and could feel the gratitude and love he felt for his daughters. He was a short stocky man, about 5'9" but his presence was obvious.

"You take care of yourself and keep in touch. We'll stay in town until Cassie's ready to travel. Don't worry about Mandy, we'll make her understand."

I shook his hand then headed to the car. I had no idea how I would find Damien, all I knew was Southern Nevada but I had no idea where. Damien said I would know when I saw his face but I didn't see his face, I saw mine. I sat in the driver's seat and tried to communicate with him again. Nothing. I'm on my own for now.

I sat there for a few moments and thought of Mandy. She was going to be so mad and may never forgive or trust me again. I had to remind myself that she would be alive and safe. I had a perfect picture of Mandy's face in my mind when my face jumped out at me!

"What is going on?!" *Then a road sign flashed in place of my face and it read "Pahrump 20 miles" then it turned to a county road sign with the number 85.* Now maybe we're getting somewhere. I'm supposed to drive to Pahrump, Nevada then find Cty. Road 85. *"Well, that's a start."* I checked the map, put the car in gear and headed for Pahrump.

Damien

I found my way to Pahrump and passed the sign that told me "Pahrump 20 miles". I took the first exit and found a gas station to top off the tank and get a map. I asked the guy behind the counter the quickest way to the county road. It didn't take long to find the road and there was a sign for an airport which had to be the one Damien sent to my brain. That had to be where they held him captive. The sign for the airport said 15 miles and this county road was very deserted and kind of creepy. The landscape was extremely flat and barren. I could see for miles in every direction. I decided to pull over about eight miles from the airport and try to contact Damien. I closed my eyes and concentrated. It must've worked this time because my head began that painful pounding and my mind went completely black for a few seconds and then....

"You're here, I can see you! Okay Jesse we have to be very careful. They've drugged me just enough to make me

weak and still have me strapped to this stupid bed but I think once you get the straps off I can get up on my own, I hope. Can you see me?"

"I see the hangar. There's three men outside the main door smoking and talking. I can't see you but I recognize one of them, it was the one that kept Mandy from being attacked by that pig. I'm going to jump into his brain and see if I can 'hear' their plan. I'll be right back." For some reason, I didn't even have to think about how to go from Damien's head to the thug who helped Mandy.

"I cannot believe we are still at this! When is this Jesse supposed to be here with the girls? And when is TJ making his appearance?"

"Mike, I don't know when TJ will be here but he wants us to be ready because that guy and the two girls should be here anytime. How he knows that I have no idea. Let's go into the office and go over the plan one more time." The vile female thug, Brandi, seemed to know more than Mike this time. That was a switch. Brandi had walked out of the hangar to join the three men outside then all four went into this small room just inside the hangar door to the left. Three more thugs joined them in the office. That meant there were seven.

"We have to be careful because TJ is certain that the guy we have here has transferred his powers to this Jesse guy that rescued the girls. He must have because none of us saw him coming. Okay, the words just came out of my mouth but it still seems so stupid. Powers, give me a break! What are we, in the Twilight Zone?" Brandi threw her arms in the air.

I was just about to find Damien's head when mine began to throb no, explode through my temples. My mind went black for what seemed like hours but must've been seconds. Then images began to race, they were moving so fast I couldn't tell what was happening at first. I couldn't think rationally then horror filled my entire being. The background in my head went from rushing images to red. The red started at the top and dripped down slowly as if someone dumped a bucket of blood from the top of my mind and let it flow down to the bottom.

I tried to get out of this vision or whatever it was but my head hurt worse and the red became more intense the harder I tried. The background began to swirl around but seemed to get lighter in color until it disappeared completely and I was standing, in my vision, in the hangar.

I stood in the middle of the room terrified. I looked around without moving my body, just turning my head. Mutilated bodies lie on the floor, blood surrounding each of them. As I began to turn in all directions I counted seven bodies, six males and one female. They were the guards, thugs, bandits whatever one would call the kidnappers. Their bodies were badly ripped apart! I still couldn't move and then it hit me, Damien! My legs and feet felt like they were cemented to the ground but I managed to move toward Damien's room carefully stepping around the bodies. When I cleared the murders I was able to walk a little faster, lighter and could see his door ahead of me. I came to the opening of the door and was about to peer in when the vision stopped as abruptly as it began.

I sat in the vehicle trembling and sweating. I brought my hand up to start the ignition but the shaking of my right hand was so intense I couldn't get it to cooperate. My head began to pound again but it wasn't a vision this time, it was Damien.

"Jesse! JESSE! Something's happening but I can't tell what's going on. There's screaming and things breaking, I can't move! Jesse you need to get in here now! NOW!"

"Okay I'm on my way!" I forced my right hand to cooperate this time. The engine ignited and I sped up to the hangar. I knew I was about to see my vision turn into reality and if I hurried maybe I could see what killed the kidnappers. On the other hand, they, it or whatever is could capture me as well. I had to find out and get Damien out of there.

I pulled the car to side of the building and found a window. I didn't want to go in there blind but the damage was already done. How could the murderers have gotten out so quickly? I ran around to the main door and in the middle of the hangar was my vision. Exactly as I saw it but instead of standing there I immediately went to Damien's room. I called his name out loud since all the kidnappers were dead but there was no answer. Could he be dead also? Please God, no. I slowly peered around the corner and saw him lying on the hospital bed. I couldn't see his face, the bed pointed to the door but his head was on the other end and he was covered in a sheet. I didn't see any blood so I cautiously walked closer. I could see the straps that had him confined.

"Damien, are you okay?" I waited for a response before getting any closer.

"I'm fine but we need to get the hell out of here. What happened out there? I tried getting into any of their heads but there was too much chaos and I couldn't enter. Get me out of these straps." He started struggling but the drugs they had him on didn't allow him to move very well. I didn't answer his questions right away, I wanted to concentrate on getting the both of us back to the car. I pulled the sheet off which revealed the straps that confined his hands, they looked like the straps used in psych wards. I quickly started taking the arm bands off but hadn't looked at his face yet. I got his left hand unbound and turned to head around to the other side of the bed for his right hand. I caught a glimpse of his face and stopped dead in my tracks. I backed up and took another look. Damien didn't seem surprised by my shock. I stood there staring and at first I couldn't speak but the urgency of our situation allowed Damien to speak for me.

"Jesse, we're identical twins. I'll explain on the way out of this hell hole. Get me out of here."

"We're what?! That's impossible! What the hell are you talking about....?!"

"Jesse! Seriously we've got to get out of here!" I snapped out of it for the time being and returned to my original goal, getting us out of danger. I removed all the straps and bands on his hands and feet and helped Damien sit up. They had him in a hospital gown. He slowly swung his legs around to the edge of the bed and kept his left arm around my shoulder for support. I noticed slippers on the floor and helped him to his feet. He was very wobbly but managed to put his feet into the slippers.

"The slippers are for walking to the bathroom, that's the only time they let me up. Now let's get the hell out of Dodge!"

I held Damien tight as we entered the hangar forgetting he hadn't seen the carnage that lay on the floor. It was

Damien's turn for shock and shocked he was. I snapped him out of it this time and we continued our way out of the building. I kept my eyes open for the monster or monsters that were responsible for this massacre. The vehicle was close thank goodness. We moved as quickly as Damien's feet would allow and when we got to the passenger's side his feet began to slide on the gravel. I managed to recover his balance and clumsily get him into the seat. I slammed the door and ran around the front of the truck losing my grip on the gravel and hit the ground on my left side. I scrambled to my feet and jumped into the driver's side. The truck seemed to understand the emergency and turned over quickly when I turned the ignition key.

I put the truck in drive and took one last look at the hangar door when I saw them again! Piercing, bright red eyes staring back at us! I couldn't see the body attached to the eyes but it was daylight and I could see how large this creature must be. The eyes were at least five feet off the ground but I couldn't tell if it was a two or four legged creature. Maybe it was 20 legs, I didn't know. That was three times seeing these eyes. I began to wonder if this 'thing' was protecting us. Interesting.

"Jesse let's go! What are you waiting for?!"

"Okay, sorry. We're outta here!" I decided to keep the 'eyes' to myself for the time being as I figured he'd had enough trauma for one lifetime.

"Damien, call the police and tell them we're on our way to the hospital. Tell them about the dead kidnappers. Then you have some serious explaining to do." I handed him my cell phone.

"How many bodies did you see?"

"Seven, six males and one female."

"Crap, we're not completely out of danger. TJ is still out there." Damien's gaze was distant but he snapped himself out of it and dialed 911. He explained to Dispatch what had happened and told them we'd meet the officers at the hospital. Dispatch told him they'd send some units out to the hangar as well along with the Coroner.

"Who is TJ? I 'heard' the thugs talk about him. I figured he was the big kahoona but do you know him?"

"I'll tell ya later, let's just get out of here."

We sped down the gravel road to the main road that led to the highway. It was about an hour drive back to the girls which would give Damien and I some time to have a question and answer session.

"Okay now that we're somewhat out of danger, start talking. Let's start at the end then you can explain why it is that we look exactly alike. Start with these powers and that letter. I have been racking my brain and still cannot figure out how you pulled that one off." I caught my breath and let him start.

"What letter?" Damien looked at me with a giant question mark.

"What do you mean what letter'?! The letter that got me involved in this entire mess!"

"Jesse I'm serious, I have no idea what you're talking about."

"The letter from Cassie asking you for help that turned up at my house instead. I wrote 'return to sender' put it in the mailbox and the next day it was delivered to me by a service. Then I threw it in the garbage, put the can in the garage and had a nightmare or vision or something that night and it was physically in my hand again! And if that wasn't creepy enough, your voice came over the television and told me to help rescue the girls! THAT LETTER!"

"Jesse, that was my voice on the television, it was the only way I could contact you at first. They had me so drugged up that I couldn't locate you and when I did I was too weak to enter your head completely. When I finally did get into your head I still wasn't able to communicate so, and I'm still not sure how I did that but I was able to communicate through the TV. A letter, I really don't know what you're talking about. Do you still have it?"

"Yep, it's in my bag in the backseat." Damien reached around and found the letter in my duffel bag. That had also reminded him to find out about the papers he wanted me to guard with my life. I told him the location of the folder and he grabbed that as well. He seemed to relax when he had the papers in his possession again. He read the letter and ended up with more questions that of course, I couldn't answer. I expected him to be the wise one with all the answers. We decided to table the letter topic and moved on.

"How did you obtain these abilities and how the hell are you able to transfer them to someone else?"

"I'm a Biologist and I spent time in southern Brazil doing research. I traveled there on a research ship. We passed an island that I felt compelled to explore. I convinced the captain to turn the ship around and drop me off. That took some convincing and truthfully, he could've lost his job for that one. For some reason, which I still can't explain, I was drawn to this island. I felt as if a huge hand was pulling at me.

The ship was to pass by in three days to pick me up but as usual when I'm involved in my work, I lose track of time; days, weeks even months. I stumbled on a tribe deep in the forest and thought for sure they would kill me. Luckily, they took me in and after a few weeks of learning their traditions and some of their language I discovered another intriguing fact about them. One day the chief took me aside and after hours of our language barrier he communicated that he wanted me to become one of them, sort of. I was thrilled as it would enhance my research and went along. Since I couldn't understand most of what they were doing or saying, I just trusted they knew what was best. I don't know another way to explain that. It was like hallucinating on drugs. Well, you know exactly what I went through. You experienced the same thing when I transferred them to you." Damien took a deep breath. Dredging up these memories must be difficult. He looked straight ahead out the windshield and continued.

"We spent the next few months training and honing all the new powers. Since we couldn't talk per say; the chief showed me my new found abilities. We were going to begin the understanding of why the abilities exist when I began having vivid, horrific nightmare; mutilated bodies and large quantities of blood. I had dreams of these ominous crimson eyes staring at me through bushes or at a distance up the beach. I never saw the body attached to the eyes. They just watched and I couldn't tell from the nightmares if the creature or whatever it was wanted to stalk me before killing me or....protect me."

"Wait, crimson eyes? I've seen those eyes! The first time was in some brush outside the house where the girls were being held. A second time whatever it was opened the locked window for me to enter the house and all I saw were the eyes. While inside the house I got this weird feeling that I was being watched. The last time was a few minutes at the hangar right before we left. I saw the eyes inside the hangar door! Could those be the eyes that you had nightmares about?! Did you ever see them when you were awake?"

"I did actually. I finally got so freaked out by the whole experience that I crept away one night. I decided it was time to get the hell out of there while I could. I had a small boat stashed on the beach and it took me awhile to find my way in the dark but I did finally make it. I felt I wasn't alone and was being watched. It scared me because I thought one of the tribes' people had followed me and was going to kill me for escaping. The whole time I was on the island I never felt frightened until those last few nights when the nightmares began.

When I dragged the boat to the water I glanced up the beach to the foliage and saw the eyes staring at me. Well, that did it! I jumped in the boat, flipped it around and headed out to sea. I was lucky that it was a very calm night and even luckier when a yacht came sailing by and picked me up.

When I got back to the states I contacted my boss. I was lucky to still have a job and of course he wanted all of my journals. I kept putting him off as I wanted to go through them first then all this craziness started and the journals are still with me.

I asked him if the ship captain lost his job because of my stupidity. I was relieved when he told me that he was put on probation but did not lose his job and was doing fine. I convinced my boss to give me the phone number so I could apologize. The captain was pissed at me but after several minutes of me gravelling, he forgave me." Damien stopped and started flipping through his paperwork. I decided to give him a few minutes to gather his thoughts before asking him the tougher questions. He was a little out of it from being drugged.

We sat silent for a few more minutes then he continued with the "beginning of our lives" story. We still had about thirty minutes before reaching the hospital. The whole time he talked I kept looking away from the road for a few seconds to glance at this mystery sitting beside me. I listened to everything he told me but my biggest question lurked in the air. Finally he began again....

"I've known about you since I was 12. Jesse, our so called father was evil. I overheard him telling one of his drunken friends one day the whole story. When he found out our mom was having twins he beat her, hoping one of us or both of us would die. When that didn't work, he found a dirty lawyer who sold you to your adoptive parents. Your parents thought everything was legit and Jesse, you definitely got the best of that world. Our father was a horrible abusive man and a mean drunk.

When we were born he paid off the doctor to lie to our mom. He, Petros was our so called father's name, had all the arrangements with the slimy lawyer before we were born. Our mom, Trina, was told that one of the twins died at birth.

Tracy Plehn

Over the years I've talked to friends of hers that tried getting her out of the situation even before she got pregnant. She would finally agree, he would find out and beat her until she promised not to leave him." Damien sighed heavily before continuing.

"When I was two years old the bastard beat her so bad that she died. He told everyone and the police that she ran off and disappeared. They all bought it, idiots. He admitted to his drunken friend that he burned the body in a field. The authorities never found her remains. As soon as I heard that monster admit all of this, I could feel tears coming but didn't want the drunken fools to hear me so I choked them down. I wanted to hear the rest of this nightmare. He was investigated but since there was no body they couldn't prove foul play.

He eventually drank himself to death a few years back. Good riddance, the world is a better place now." Damien's eyes were glistening from tears. I couldn't speak and just stared out the windshield. I'm surprised we even made it to town; I don't remember any landmarks or signs. I have no idea how I found the hospital with all these images of Damien and our mother being beat by this twisted sore excuse of a human being. It's a good thing he's dead, I probably would've killed him myself. I didn't even know I was adopted! I couldn't wrap my head around everything.

<u>Chapter Seven</u>

We pulled into a parking space and I shut the engine off. We both sat there in a dead silence.

"How did you turn out so normal, at least from where I sit you seem normal."

"When Petros finally met his maker down below the authorities put me in a foster home, I was 14. It was the best thing that could've happened to me. This family was upper middle-class and very kind people. I don't know how they put up with me at first. I was mouthy and kept getting into trouble. When I hit high school something inside of me snapped. I realized, not sure how, that I needed to break the cycle and make a better life for myself. I got a swimming scholarship to college. Eleven years later, here I am." We got out of the truck and headed into the hospital. Reality set in and I decided to snap out of my trance before seeing Mandy.

"I hope Mandy forgives me for leaving without her." I explained Cassie's condition to Damien again so he'd be mentally prepared. I had called their dad when we hit the highway and let him know Damien was okay and we were on our way back. I had only been gone for a few hours but it seemed like days. So much had happened.

Damien and I found our way to Cassie's room. Their mother and Mandy were sitting by her side. Their dad must've forewarned Mandy that I was on my way because her expression was priceless, relief. She jumped up to run to me but stopped midway. Her facial expression changed to anger and it was so cute that I had to choke down a laugh. I loved it when she got angry because she couldn't pull it off. Her face turned red then to shock as she realized she was seeing double! I was pretty sure if Damien hadn't been through such an ordeal and scruffy looking, Mandy wouldn't be able to tell us apart.

"What, wait...HUH?! You're Damien?! How could this.... you didn't tell me you were twins!" She was standing in the middle of the room looking at Damien. I walked over and gave her a hug.

"Skittles, I didn't know anything about this. I was adopted and didn't even know that until a few minutes ago! It's a long story and Damien will explain later but let's give him a few minutes with Cassie. I also want the doc to check him out." Damien shook their mom's hand and introduced himself. I couldn't tell if she was relieved he was okay or angry that he got their babies into this mess. She was probably feeling both emotions.

She came over and hugged me again then walked out of the room.

"Wait! I'm very mad at you! How could you leave without me? You promised! You could have been killed and I never would've seen....UGH!" As she read me the riot act, I gently pulled at her elbow to lead her out of Cassie's room and into the hallway. She was still quietly rambling when we arrived at the cafeteria. I had become very hungry when we got to the hospital.

It was dinner time and there were a few people in line. Neither of us spoke for awhile, I just held her in my arms and didn't want to let go. As the line moved, we moved as one. I was so happy that she wasn't so angry that she didn't want to be around me.

"Mandy, I know Damien and I have a lot of explaining to do but just for tonight can we get a hotel room and just be free to be with each other? No danger, no voices or visions; just us." She hugged me tighter and nodded her head. I heard a rustling noise and realized she had pulled out a bag of Skittles from her pocket. I had to chuckle.

When we finished eating we went up to Cassie's room to explain to her parents and Damien our plans for the night. They assured us they would call if there was any change. They said they would probably be going back to the hotel as well and would take Damien with them.

We made our way to the hotel where her parents were staying, a few miles away. It wasn't one of the big chains but very nice. I got us a suite which had a king size bed; huge walk-in closet; large living area with a flat screen TV; and a big bathroom with a Jacuzzi tub. We put our bags on the bed and Mandy started taking out some things but

I could tell she was going through the motions. I stood next to her and just watched, admired. She stopped taking items out for a second and stood frozen. I wasn't sure if I should be worried that she came to her senses and decided she hated me.

"Jesse, it just hit me. You're okay!" She wheeled around and grabbed my face bringing it down to hers. Her touch was so urgent. Our lips met and the silkiness of hers made my entire body feel like it was on fire. She still had her eyes open as if she expected me to disappear again. I gently grabbed her shoulders and pulled her away a micro inch and looked into those begging eyes.

"Mandy, I'm not going anywhere. You seized my heart and soul the second I laid eyes on you." We stood there for a moment then passion filled our hearts. Mandy took hold of my shirt from the bottom and slipped it over my head and where it landed is anybody's guess. She never took her eyes off mine. She began to run her hands down my chest when I took her shirt from the bottom and slipped it over her head. My heart skipped, I don't know, a thousand beats. She wore a light pink lacy bra and I unlatched it without difficulty. She let it slide off her arms to the floor, still gazing into my eyes. Her look went from worry to 'I need you now'.

We began kissing again and melted onto the bed. We intertwined until the passion took hold with an iron grip. Mandy's touch, supple skin and the petite curves of her body would've driven an insane man deeper into oblivion. I couldn't get close enough or feel enough of her body. I wanted every inch of her to be a part of me. I had made love before but never like this not this kind of love and passion. I had never felt this intense or protective of anyone. I knew at that moment that I would lay my life down for this woman and if anyone ever hurt her well, I would end up in prison. I was gone, this was it for me.

Afterward, we stayed intertwined and tried desperately to catch our breath. Every blood cell in my body was gasping for air and sweat dripped from both of us. We laid there for awhile then decided to take a Jacuzzi bath. I told Mandy to stay in bed and I would get the bath ready. I made the excuse of getting some colas and went downstairs to see if the front desk would have candles. The gal behind the counter surprised me with three scented candles, perfect. I was about to reach for our door knob when I realized I forgot the sodas. I turned around and got two out of the machine in the little vending area down the hall.

Mandy was still awake and lying on her back on top of the covers. She had been staring at the ceiling with her arms folded and tucked behind her head. I stood there for a second looking at every curve. Her breasts lay perfectly on her chest and her stomach was slightly concave which showed her beautiful hip bones. She realized I was standing there and got a little embarrassed.

"I didn't hear you Scooby." Her delicate face turned red.

"I didn't mean to scare you but I couldn't help watching you. You are so beautiful. What were you thinking about?"

"Everything. I feel like I'm going to jump out of my skin! I'm thinking about my sister and how relieved I am she's going to be okay. I'm thinking about you and you're safe and here with me. I'm thinking about how much I love you. I've never felt this way about anyone and it's scaring me. I can't get enough of you! I'm thinking about Damien; which brings me back to thinking of you and you two are twins! You're twins like me and Cassie! How bizarre is that?! Did Cassie even know? How did you not know? What's going to happen next? And…" I had to cut her off before she hyperventilated. She was talking so fast and I tried to be polite and not interrupt but I really did worry that she would pass out.

"Skittles, all in good time. Let's take a bath and relax. Damien and I will explain everything in the morning. I'm still processing everything myself but tonight is about you and me, nothing else matters." She smiled a full 'melt in my skin' smile and I motioned for her to stay in bed a few more moments. I slipped into the bathroom and started the bath. There was rose scented bubble bath that rested on the side of the tub, quite feminine but this was for Mandy who was the definition of feminine.

I walked toward the bed and with my right index finger told her to come with me. She slid off the bed and followed me into the bathroom. I got into the tub first then taking her left hand, I helped her in. She sat with her back to me and between my legs. The jet streams felt like heaven on our bodies. I had lit the three candles and dimmed the lights. The bathroom filled with rosebud and lilac aromas. I desperately wished this moment would never end. We laid wrapped in each other's arms and legs. I could've stayed like this until we looked like wrinkled raisins. It felt so natural and calming to have her in my arms. But leave it to Skittles, the detective, to break the silence.

"So, what powers do you have? How did you get them and does Damien have them as well?" She was swirling the fingers of her left hand in the water while resting her arms on my knees. I knew the wheels had been turning in her mind but I forced myself not to read her mind, I had gotten good at tuning in and out of peoples' thoughts.

"No! Tomorrow."

"Fine! I'll just have to be patient and as you can tell, that's not my forte." She sat very still and quiet for a few seconds and I almost 'tuned in' to her thoughts but hesitated. All of a sudden she reached down to my right foot and started tickling it. Unfortunately, that's the only part of my body that is ticklish. I grabbed her wrists and started tickling her ribs. Well, that was a mistake because water went all over the floor as we sloshed around in the tub. It was awesome to hear full laughter sounds come bellowing out of her.

"Okay, okay, Uncle! I give, stop!" I stopped and folded my arms around her and held on tight. Then a ringing sound came from the other room, her phone. She jumped out of the water and quickly wrapped a towel around her while running for her phone.

"Hello.....Okay, we'll be right there!" She burst through the bathroom with tears in her eyes.

"Baby, what's wrong?"

"Nothing! She's awake! C'mon let's go." We both dressed with lightning speed and raced to the hospital. Everyone was in Cassie's room surrounding her bed. Damien, their parents the doctor and two nurses. The nurses noticed us bursting through the door and made way for Mandy to be at her bedside. Mandy gently put her arms around her sister's neck and sobbed.

"Hey baby sister I'm okay. A little sore but that's it." Cassie hugged her back and didn't try to hold the tears back.

"Oh my God, you have no idea how scared we were! Here you are, awake! Oh, am I hurting you?" Mandy realized she may be squeezing too tight and jumped back.

"Not at all. It's mostly my ribs that hurt but the doc says everything is going to heal perfectly. We Tagama's, we're tough you know." She winked at Mandy then grabbed Damien's hand who had been sitting on the other side of the bed across from Mandy. Damien leaned down to give her a light hug. Cassie glanced at me at the end of her bed. I was trying to stay out of the way. I wasn't sure if Damien had told Cassie about the whole "twin" thing yet and I wondered if she would remember the two of us 'talking' to each other while she was unconscious. I wanted to listen to her thoughts but decided against it.

"Oh my God, it's so good to see all of you! I prayed every day for this moment and here it is and here you all are!" Cassie's eyes wandered over Damien's shoulder while he hugged her. Damien straightened himself and stood up. He knew what was coming next.

Jesse, I didn't have a chance to tell Cassie about us yet. Get ready.

Okay, but I forgot to tell you that she and I had a conversation while she was under. She couldn't see me but I don't know if she will remember. Damien didn't have time to respond.

"Dad, it's good to see you!" Their father joined their mother who was standing next to Mandy.

"Baby Doll you have no idea how happy your mother and I are to have you back!"

"Dad, I think I do have an idea because you have no idea how happy I am to be here with all of you!" Then Cassie's head turned back to the end of her bed where I stood by myself. *Okay Jesse, here it comes.* I thought to myself.

"So, you must be Jesse? I'm assuming you're the one I talked to or what do I call it, telepathy? I don't understand how you do what Damien does and I didn't know you guys are twins. I do know that I owe you my life. Jesse, thank you for saving me and my sister." Tears started streaming down her face so I decided to lighten the mood.

"Aw shucks M'aam, it ain't nothin'." I winked at her and Mandy reached over and took my left hand.

"Alright everyone, time is up. This young lady needs some rest." The doctor came into the room. Damien told Cassie he'd be right back and motioned the doctor out to the hallway. I heard the concern in Damien's voice. Another one of these abilities was uncanny hearing.

"Is she really going to be okay or is there something you're not telling us?"

153

"She will make a full recovery. I would like to keep her for one or two more days but I don't see why she couldn't go home after that." He shook Damien's hand.

We all, including her parents, decided to head to the cafeteria and grab a bite. I still had some questions for Damien which of course would start a barrage of questions from Mandy. I felt for him but I wanted mine answered too. I'm sure her parents had some of their own for both of us. We found a booth and Damien and I went up to the counter to get food for everyone.

"Damien there's still a lot I want to know and I know you're exhausted but one question in particular is nagging at me. Who were the kidnappers and what did they want? Your powers?"

"Yep. TJ, the leader so to speak, used to be my best friend. We grew up together and stayed friends through college and until now, we were tight. While I was on the island I had made all those journals and formulas. When I returned to the states I got together with TJ for a couple of beers and wanted to tell him of my adventures in the jungle. I told that um, well, slime bag everything. I never in a million years would've thought he would turn on me!

A few days later I got a phone call from him wanting to meet me for another beer. Sure, why not we're best buds. I needed all the down time I could get after the experiences I had on the island. I wasn't planning on returning to work to finish my research for another week or so and having some fun definitely sounded good. I was to meet him at one of the casinos, which by the way, is where Cassie and I met. She was a Black Jack dealer if you can believe that. I played some Black Jack while waiting on TJ. Cassie and I started talking. This was almost a year ago, I can't believe it. Okay, I keep digressing." He was interrupted when our food arrived on a big tray. I pushed the tray out of the way of the other customers so Damien and I could continue the conversation. We both glanced at Mandy and her parents; they were involved in their own conversation.

"TJ showed up, we had a couple beers and he asked a lot of questions about the island and wanted to know all about my abilities. I sure wish I would've 'tuned' into his thoughts from the beginning because we may not be in this mess. I don't like to do that unless absolutely necessary. TJ and I finished our conversation then Cassie and I started hanging out every day.

Months went by and I continued with my research, trying to figure out the full extent of my abilities, the pros and cons. I started feeling a little strange. At first I chalked it up to exhaustion. Between my work and spending time with Cassie, I didn't get much sleep. But it wasn't that. I think having so many abilities and trying so hard to understand them plus being exhausted started some low tolerance traits. The harder I tried to contain these traits, the worse they became. Oh, you and I will work on that before it gets bad for you. I now know how to 'exercise' them. I don't know another term for it but it would be like getting out your frustrations; maybe taking a run or lifting weights. With these abilities you have to 'stretch' them, use them so they don't implode. Does that make sense?"

"Kind of but I want to hear about TJ before Mandy motions us back to the table. Oh by the way, get ready for a gazillion questions from her. I think I can hold her off until you get some sleep but be prepared. Now continue."

"Okay. Long story short, Cassie started getting frightened from my moods and I didn't realize how bad they were. I thought she was being ridiculous and ignoring her fears, which is not like me at all. She finally got smart and kicked me out. Yes, we were living together. I didn't have much time to realize what an idiot I had been because TJ called me a few days after we broke up and wanted to start hanging out again. I met him at a casino, big surprise in Vegas to meet at casinos. I was sitting at a dollar machine when I felt his presence come into the building. I made the mistake, well thought it was a mistake, of 'hearing' his thoughts. I was about to turn it off when I 'heard' him call me a sap. He talked to himself in his head about his plan to kidnap me and force me to tell him how I got the powers, transfer them to him and show him how to use them.

I asked the waitress to do me a favor and call my phone as TJ got closer. I'm sure she thought I was nuts but it worked. I answered my phone and pretended it was an emergency with Cassie, he didn't know we broke up. I ran up to him and pretended to apologize telling him Cassie had been in a car accident, which was the quickest thing I could come up with. He bought it but I heard him cussing in his mind and decided to hold off on the plan. As I ran out of the casino I 'heard' him rattle off the people he needed to call. He needed to tell them to stand-down, the plan would be delayed. I knew of an old house that had been deserted and boarded up for years. TJ and I had never been there together so it wasn't a place he would think to look for my journals.

The house you rescued them from." Damien's attention was turned to Mandy's table as he accidentally read her thoughts.

"Ooops, she wants us back."

"Hey, quit that!" Damien grabbed the tray of food and I walked over with the glasses and got drinks for everyone. We all sat and ate, surprisingly hungry considering it was two a.m. Mandy did very well and did not ask too many questions of Damien. Her parents on the other hand, did not hold back.

Damien obliged and answered all their questions and pretty much explained everything I had heard all day and tonight. Mandy seemed to be content with those answers for now. Two hours went by and we all decided to get some sleep. Mandy and I had everyone follow us to the hotel so we could all be in one place. Mandy and I went up to our room, threw on t-shirts and collapsed exhausted.

A knock on the door startled me. I looked at the nightstand and glanced at the clock, 11:30! Wow! Half the day is gone! Mandy stirred but didn't wake up. I quietly slipped out of bed and answered the door. It was Damien and her parents explaining they were heading back to the hospital. I told them I would let Mandy sleep awhile longer and we would be there soon. Only another thirty minutes and Mandy woke up.

"Hey Skittles. Everyone went to the hospital but I wanted to let you sleep a little longer." I sat on the bed next to her and she stretched and yawned.

Tracy Plehn

"Thank you. I slept so hard, I hope I didn't snore. Do I snore?" I had to laugh.

"No Babe you were extremely quiet." I hugged her and she pulled me into the bed. We made out for a few minutes then she wanted to hop into the shower. We both got ready to leave then went down to the main desk to pay for a couple more nights.

We got to the hospital and parked next to her parents' rental car which happened to be under Cassie's window. Damien was walking out to the car as we parked.

"Hey Damien, what's up?"

"I forgot my journals and I don't want them unattended. When we get into the hospital, we need to 'find' TJ." I told Mandy to go on up and we'd be there shortly. All of a sudden I got that strange tingling sensation and every hair on my body stood at attention. I caught a glimpse of something by one of the trees that bordered the parking lot. The eyes, the daunting crimson eyes that kept appearing!

"Damien, look over by that tree! Do you see them?!" I quickly turned to Mandy and she had just turned around to wave at me, when I saw horror in her eyes. She must've seen them as well. Damien quickly looked at the tree.

"Where did it go?! Jesse have you ever seen what the eyes are attached to?"

"No. And I can't figure out if it wants to hurt us or help us. I'm sure whatever it is massacred those kidnappers

158

which definitely helped us but why? Damien, what does it want with us?"

"I don't know but right now Mandy needs some reassurance that everything is okay." He motioned his head sideways toward Mandy and I responded immediately.

"Baby, it's okay. Come on, let's get inside and see how Cassie's doing." I ran to her side and put my arm around her shoulder.

"Jesse, what was that and don't lie to me. I saw you and Damien talking about it."

"We honestly don't know but I don't think it's anything that wants to harm us. Let's not think about it right now and concentrate on your sister." Damien followed.

We arrived at Cassie's room and visited for awhile.

Jess, let's go get some sodas.

Okay. Is something wrong?

No, I want to talk about TJ and how to locate him. We told everyone we'd be right back. Mandy gave me quite the look but I reassured her I was only going to the cafeteria. We sat at a booth for a few minutes before getting the sodas.

Okay Jesse, I'm going to concentrate on TJ's face and try to locate him.

Alright and then what? Do we go after him?

I don't know, let's take it one step at a time and find him first. Mandy followed us without our knowledge and plopped herself next to me. She had guessed we were talking telepathically and got irritated.

"Stop it! I deserve to know what you guys are planning and it's not fair that you two can do that. Let me in on the plan." She crossed her arms over her chest and looked very somber.

"Sorry Babe. There's nothing to tell yet, we're trying to locate the lead kidnapper, TJ."

"I thought they were all dead at the hangar." I realized I had made a big mistake telling Mandy about TJ. I knew she would be scared from this point on until TJ was brought to justice. Me and my big mouth.

"They are but TJ used to be a friend of Damien's then turned on him. He's the one who orchestrated the whole kidnapping plan. He wasn't at the hangar. But don't worry, we're going to find him." We had been whispering so Damien wouldn't be too distracted. He had his fingers on his temples and closed his eyes tight. I decided to tap into his thought processes but that didn't go over very well.

Dammit Jesse, get out of here. I don't want to screw this up. When I find him I have to be very quiet so he can't 'hear' me. I don't want to spook him.

Okay, okay. Sorry. Do your thing and I'll mind my own business, Mr. Grumpy. Damien looked at me scowling but then smiled. Mandy hit my arm and reminded me that I would stop talking telepathically. I apologized by giving her a kiss and that seemed to calm her down.

"I found him! Wait, I can't tell if this is happening now or in the future." Damien grabbed his head and pushed himself away from the table with his feet.

"Damien, what's happening?" I knew he had gone into a vision state and there was nothing I could do until he came out of it. I didn't want to risk giving us away by 'joining' him in his vision so I stayed quiet and held Mandy's hand. She was squeezing it very tightly. Damien came out fairly quick but was terrified. He was sweating and shaking, still holding his head,

"The creature with the eyes….oh God. TJ is…he's or he's about to be…dead. I couldn't see what belonged to the eyes but I could see TJ and blood like he imploded." Damien threw his head on the table holding his temples.

"When I had the vision of the kidnappers' massacre, that happened moments before my vision, well I'm guessing. TJ's probably dead by now. Could you tell where it was?"

"No, it was too fast. It was as if I was spinning in circles while watching him implode. What is this thing and why is it killing? It's like the creature, or whatever we call it, is killing for us. Is that possible?" Mandy was trying not to freak out. I put my arm around her shoulder and pulled her close to me. She pressed herself tight into my side and listened intently to mine and Damien's conversation.

"I can't find this thing with the eyes because I can't see its face. Ugh! Okay, let's take a break and decide what we do when Cassie gets out of the hospital." I was beginning to like my brother already. *'Brother', how weird is that?*

Tracy Plehn

"Hey, I heard that Jesse." This would take a lot of getting used to. Not only did I have an identical twin but we both had powers, abilities, curses whatever one would call them and would not be able to have any secrets from each other because of these powers. It made my head spin and I hadn't had time to really let all of this soak in. Now that a lot of the danger was behind us, we hoped, I would really be able to stop and analyze some of it. That also meant that Mandy and I could really start getting to know one another and maybe have some fun. We had done things backward and fell in love before dating.

All three of us kept the conversation fun and breezy and decided to go on a vacation as soon as Cassie was given the 'okay' from her doctor to travel. I told them of my original plans for the Virgin Islands before so rudely interrupted by Damien. We all laughed and decided it was a great idea and Mandy knew Cassie would be all for it.

"How weird is this going to be? Two sets of identical twins dating each other?" Mandy had decided to be the first to say it out loud even though we all thought it.

"It will be a blast. We could really play some cruel head games on people." Damien nodded at me and winked at Mandy.

Their parents wandered down to the cafeteria looking for us. We had lunch and convinced them that everything, especially Cassie, was fine and they should head back home. They decided it was a good idea and would leave when Cassie was released. We finished eating then all headed back to Cassie's room.

Before we got to the room something occurred to me.

"Damien, did you leave your journals in the room?"

"No, I put them in the hotel safe."

"Oh, alright." We got to Cassie's room and she was channel surfing.

"Do you know how exciting it is to do something normal like channel surf?!" Damien laid on the bed with her and Mandy and I sat in the oversized chair next to the bed. I had sat down first then grabbed Mandy by her waist and pulled her down on my lap.

"Well, do you know how exciting it is to see you do something so normal?!" Mandy's eyes were beginning to tear up.

"Stop it, you'll make me cry."

"I can't help it I'm just so happy that you're okay and don't you EVER do this to me again!"

"Oh, okay. The next time someone kidnaps me I'll just tell them to take a hike because my baby sister said so."

"Cassie don't joke about it! I was scared to death and by the way, you're only older by minutes."

"Sorry. I don't mean to make light of the situation but it's the only way I can deal with it for now. And minutes or seconds, I'm still older!" They both laughed then looked at me and Damien at the exact same time. It was as if they told each other telepathically to look right...now. It was a little spooky.

"What?" I couldn't imagine why they looked at us but I knew we were about to find out.

"So, which one of you is the older brother?" Mandy's face showed she couldn't wait for the answer.

"Since I didn't know I even had a brother well, I have no idea." I said turning right to Damien.

"That would be me. I'm the old man by three minutes or that's what dear ol' dad told his drunken buddy and we know how trustworthy he was."

We all sat around joking and laughing for awhile longer. It felt good to be doing something so relaxing after the last few days we've had.

"Hey, let's make some flight and hotel reservations or should I say, add to yours Jesse?" Damien smiled. We decided to head out in two days if the doctor said Cassie would be able to travel.

ST. THOMAS, VIRGIN ISLANDS

The hotel was absolutely beautiful. Cassie did great on the flight and we knew we would have to take it easy on her. She seemed sore but was in good spirits.

"Our rooms are right next to each other facing the ocean!" Mandy left Damien and I standing at the counter and ran over to Cassie who was sitting in a chair in the lobby.

"That's great Mandy." It was obvious that Cassie needed some rest immediately. Damien and I finished checking us in and grabbed our keys. Cassie and Damien wanted to stay in for awhile and let Cassie get some sleep.

"Well, we'll be back later and meet up for dinner?" I asked the two of them and Damien agreed.

"Mandy how about that date? It may not be horseback in the mountains but what about horseback on the beach?"

"I would love that!" She gave me a hug.

We went to the front desk and asked for information on the nearest stable. We were picked up by a shuttle to the stable. The gentleman was reluctant but Mandy convinced him to let us go on our own. She was very experienced and I put my life in her hands. They had picnic packages and normally it was something that had to be booked in advance but they had several couples as no shows and we were able to have a picnic lunch.

We waited outside for the horses to be brought to us and Mandy was like a little kid in a toy store. She danced around the little area like she had ants in her pants. I really enjoyed watching her.

"Okay Scooby, here they come. Are you ready for the Beasts?" She grabbed my arm above the elbow and started pulling me forward toward the oncoming horses.

"Skittles I'm trusting you, don't let these beasts eat me."

"Would I let anything happen to you?" She grabbed the reins of the Buckskin, she called it. The man told us the name of her horse was Ben and mine was Colonel. Guess they were both boys.

I hope these two know what they're doing. I don't want a law suit. Wish I was going with them she is...Wow! What a lucky bastard. I had put my guard down from watching Mandy and tuned into this man's thoughts and really wished I hadn't. He's lucky I'm a civilized man otherwise

I would have punched him right between the eyes. I shook my head and concentrated on 'turning' it off. I was amazed how quickly I had learned to control some of the abilities that Damien had forced onto me.

The man gave us a little map and loaded her saddle bags with food and water bottles. He tied the picnic blanket to the back of my saddle then helped me climb onto my beast. Of course Mandy needed no help and had been on hers for several minutes then adjusted her own stirrups from on top of the horse! If I had done that I would have landed on my head. The man came around to me, didn't even bother with Mandy as it was obvious to him she knew what she was doing, and fixed my stirrups to fit my height. I knew why Mandy had chosen the Buckskin, it was quite a bit smaller than mine and he probably would have pitched a fit when I got on him.

We started out at a slow pace and found the long stretch of beach we were allowed to ride on. The sky was turquoise blue and not a cloud as far as the eye could see. We rode side by side for several miles then found a large fallen tree trunk. We decided that would be perfect to tie up the horses while we ate our picnic. I let Mandy tie our horses since they would definitely get free if I did it and I got the blanket and food laid out. She plopped down on the blanket beside me and we looked out on the ocean. There was absolutely nothing I needed at this moment of my life, everything was perfect. A beautiful girl who loved me and the most spectacular view anyone could ask for.

We ate our roast beef sandwiches, potato salad and brownies. There was a candy machine in the lobby of the hotel and it actually had Skittles so I had snuck over and bought a couple bags. Mandy sat on my right and she leaned over to give me a kiss. Her right hand bumped my front pocket and she heard crackling.

"What do you have in your pocket?" She reached into my left front pocket and retrieved one of the bags. I just grinned.

"Aw, that's so sweet. I completely forgot to bring some to the island. Where did you find these?" She ripped it open and popped a couple in her mouth.

"That's my secret but suffice it to say, you will have plenty of Skittles while on this trip." I pulled her over and she sat in front of me between my legs. I wrapped my arms around her and we swayed side to side. Mandy turned her head as far as she could and wanted a kiss. I wasn't about to turn her down and responded by kissing back. It didn't take long for her to turn around facing me but stayed between my legs. I gently put my hands on her cheeks and stroked them with my fingertips. Our lips seemed to fit perfectly together and I could feel the temperature in my body begin to rise. I kept my hands on her face until I knew how far she wanted to go.

Mandy put her hands on my chest and pushed me onto my back. We both went down and she stayed on top of me. She raised herself up, supporting herself with her hands on either side of my chest and stared at me longingly.

"Um, do you think other people might show up?" I knew what she was asking.

"I have a solution. Are you sure the horses are tied well?"

"Uh hello, I tied them!" She laughed and sat up.

"You put your swimsuit on under your clothes right?" She knew immediately where I was going with that question and jumped up. She threw her shirt on the blanket and shorts on top of it. She was halfway to the water before I got to my feet.

"Hurry up slow poke!" She ran across the sand on the balls of her tiny feet. She was so light as she ran that the impact of her steps barely made a print in the white sand. I couldn't take my eyes off of her, she was absolutely amazing. But I snapped out of it and threw off my t-shirt and shorts. They landed on top of her clothes. I ran into the water with her and she threw her arms around my neck and wrapped her legs around my waist. Mandy loved life and I loved her for that.

We kissed passionately for several minutes. I kept her body wrapped around mine and waded deeper into the water. I untied her top and she took off the bottom half of her suit. I actually thought ahead and tied both pieces of her swim suit together and wrapped them around my arm so it wouldn't get taken out to sea. I took my suit off and put my other arm through the leg and waist. We meshed together perfectly like puzzle pieces. At that moment, we were the only two people on earth. A couple of times I put my guard down and caught some thoughts from her then shook it off. I was happy to know the real truth for once and knew she enjoyed herself as much as I did.

Afterward, we stood in the water staring into each other's eyes as the low waves pushed us back and forth.

"Mandy, I have never felt this way about anyone. I love you very much."

"I love you too Jesse." She put her head on my chest and had her arms wrapped around me, she hugged me tight.

"Maybe we should dry off and get the horses back. I want to check on Cassie." I untied our suits and we put them on in the water then I scooped her up. She locked her arms around my neck and I cradled her in my arms to the blanket on the sand. We gathered the blanket and leftover food and put them in the appropriate places on the horses. Colonel was pawing the sand with his front hoof. Figures it was my beast that was impatient. Ben looked half asleep, maybe we should trade horses. Mandy was gentle with me and kept the horses at a walk back to the stable.

The shuttle returned us to the hotel and we headed to the fourth floor to our rooms. Mandy put her ear to Damien and Cassie's door to see if she could hear anything, we didn't want to wake them but really wanted to know how Cassie was. Mandy knocked quietly and Damien answered the door.

"Hi guys. Did you have fun?"

"Yes, we had a great time. How's Cassie?" Mandy was trying to whisper in case Cassie was sleeping.

"She's good. She's been asleep this whole time."

"Well how about if we go take a shower then we'll check in with you in a couple hours for dinner?" Damien looked at me while I asked the question I could see worry in his eyes.

Damien is there something wrong?

169

I don't know, just a feeling that hit me about an hour ago. I can't put my finger on it but something's wrong. Let's keep this to ourselves, I don't want to worry the girls.

Okay.

Mandy and I took a shower together, we couldn't get enough of each other. It was only 3:30 so we laid together on the bed channel surfing. We both must have fallen asleep because we jumped when there was a knock at the door.

"Just a second." I jumped up and noticed it was almost 6! Damien and Cassie stood at the door with Cassie looking rejuvenated.

"C'mon guys, I'm starving." Cassie said as she pushed her way through the door.

"Okay Miss Bossy." Mandy told her as she stuck her tongue out at her sister. They giggled and gathered Mandy's purse.

We took a cab into town and found the restaurant the front desk recommended. It was a restaurant and bar combination. The hostess said it would only be about 20 minutes so we had drinks and made plans for tomorrow while we waited. After dinner Mandy and I danced to some steel drum music. I knew Mandy felt a little guilty since Cassie couldn't do too much but Cassie insisted we have fun. It didn't take much convincing. We sat at the restaurant until 9:30 then all decided to retire for the night.

The next morning we wanted to spend time with Damien and Cassie so we all had breakfast and the rest of the day we would hang out at the beach. It was another perfect day with bright blue sky and hot. We found a spot on the beach. We had gotten a large blanket from the front desk of the hotel and laid it out on the sand. The four of us sat there looking out over the ocean. I felt all the stress and worry from the last few days drift out of me and wash into the ocean. The girls decided to get us some drinks from the beach bar up the little hill.

"Scooby we'll be right back."

"Okay, we'll be here waiting so patiently and I'll miss you so much!" Even I couldn't keep a straight face on that one.

"Gag! Get a room you guys!" Cassie said while laughing.

"We have a room." Cassie was standing behind me and I leaned back to smack her on the foot as I said that.

"I'm thirsty, let's go. Guys we'll be right back." Mandy gently tugged on Cassie's arm to get her moving.

"How weird is this whole thing? I find out I'm an identical twin, find the love of my life who happens to be a twin of the love of your life!" It was mind boggling and I thought I'd get a good laugh from Damien but when I looked at him he didn't look as if he were breathing.

Shhh.

Damien, what is it? As soon as the words came out of my thoughts I got the prickly feeling over my entire being. Damien and I turned our heads at the same time to find the girls. We found them quickly with their backs to us but to the left of them about 100 feet between the ocean and the beach bar were the crimson eyes. It didn't move and even though it stood in the open we couldn't see the

171

body of this creature. It blinked twice, I knew something was about to happen. We had to get to the girls!

I turned to Damien and he had disappeared. Just as I was about to turn back to Mandy and Cassie and tell them to run, I was stopped by something sharp grabbing my shoulders! Then it wrapped something under my armpits and lifted me into the air! My body swayed side to side as we flew and then my foot hit something. I looked down and could see the ground about 20, 30 feet, crap I couldn't tell how high I just knew we continued to climb. My hand touched something.

"Damien, is that you?"

"Yes. I don't know what the hell is going on! I can't see you. Whatever has us made us invisible!" We wrapped our arms together for support. There was a swooshing sound like giant wings. I looked down and could see the girls and heard Mandy yelling my name but we kept climbing so I couldn't yell back. I did the next best thing and hoped it would work.

Mandy I will find a way back to you, I promise. I don't know what's going on but please take Cassie and get both of you back to the ranch. We will find our back somehow, some day. I love you. I didn't know if she heard me but I had to hope and pray she did. I couldn't read her thoughts, why?! *Oh God please don't take me from her again!* Damien heard my thoughts, my pleas and squeezed my arm for reassurance.

"We'll find our way back to our girls, I promise. And Jesse?"

"Yeah?"

"I'm so sorry."

"For what?" I was pretty sure I knew what he would say but he really didn't have anything to apologize for. I was certain that none of this was his fault.

"For getting you into this." I squeezed his arm above his elbow to reassure him that I was fine.

"Damien those eyes have something to do with what's going on. Where is this thing taking us?"

"I don't know but hang in there brother, we'll be okay. I just found you, I'm not losing you now!"

We ended up above the clouds but low enough for oxygen. It had to be hours before we could feel this thing start to descend.

"Oh my God."

"Damien, what is it?"

"The island! We're back at the island!"

"What?! Why?" We broke through some thick trees and were flying about ten feet off the ground. I thought for sure we were going to hit a tree head on. The creature flew in and out and around trees with such grace, obviously used to this kind of daredevil acrobats. Without any warning it dropped us and we landed with a hard jolt to a clearing in the trees.

It was a small clearing surrounded by heavy foliage. We both got our footing and checked each other for any broken bones. Then Damien stood straight up and froze.

"Hello Mr. Damien, welcome back. We been expecting you." His English wasn't the best but what do you expect from a tribesman. Damien bowed his head slightly and shook the chief's hand. A noise from behind us interrupted the reunion. We whipped around and there again were the crimson eyes! All six of our eyes stared at each other, not moving or breathing.

It stepped out of the foliage. It wasn't the creature that brought us here but it was the same eyes that kept peering at us. As its body emerged further out into the clearing I about had a heart attack. It showed its body this time and it was gigantic! As it came toward us Damien and I took a few steps back but bumped into something. We turned around and discovered the creature that brought us here. It looked like a giant owl only evil. Its talons had to be 10 feet long! Damien and I took three steps back from it, which meant closer to the other creature with the crimson eyes but we didn't think of that, and looked up. I estimated about 5 stories high was the flying creature's head and it looked down at us without moving. It was the head of an owl, the wings had to be 20 feet long and the body was that of an eagle maybe. All I knew was this thing was huge and ugly!

We turned back around to the other creature. It was definitely a Black Panther but colossal in size. The size reminded me of five huge Grizzly Bears in one. It was massive but beautiful. Its coat looked like silk and the shine from it about blinded us. The eyes were piercing and paralyzing. Its chest had to be four feet wide and the muscles on his shoulders rippled all the way to his huge paws. His mouth was slightly open. His teeth were ivory colored and the tongue was pink. A small amount of drool fell to the ground. At that moment, I thought we were going to be his dinner. We all stood staring at each other.

Then it morphed, it actually morphed! I felt like I was in a B rated horror movie! Its body went from a black gleaming and blinding beauty to a distortion that was indescribable. We were like deer in the headlights, we couldn't move or breathe. It stood on its hind legs as it was changing and his feet turned into male human feet with the legs and torso following turning into a human male. Its head remained a Panther until the end; a giant Black Panther head on top of a normal human body. "Normal" what a joke! Nothing about my life in the last few days has been normal! It was as if the creature was playing with us and kept his head a secret. It remained part human and part Panther. I guess the suspense was too hard for him and the head began to morph into human shape. Damien and I grabbed each others' shoulders.

"What the...? How can this be?!" Damien stammered the words then I felt his shoulder muscle go limp and he almost fell to the ground. I grabbed him under his arm and pulled him to his feet not taking my eyes off the creature, human; I didn't know what to call it. The three of us stood there staring at each other a few minutes longer then 'it' spoke.

"Hi there brothers! I've been waiting years for this moment and finally all three of us are reunited, well united. Damien, it took you long enough to find Jesse. I thought you'd never figure things out. You drove me crazy! I gave you hint after hint and still, nothing. But with a little push from me here we all are. Isn't it wonderful?! Oh, where are my manners? Let me introduce myself,

I am your triplet Nikias. This fine feathered friend behind you is Buzzard. He was our transportation to paradise." He spoke with a condescending tone then laughed………

EPILOGUE

MIST AND VENGEANCE

Chapter One

Mandy

I turned to wave at Jesse from the beach bar and he started to wave then stopped. He turned his gaze to the left of us. I looked over but didn't see anything then looked back at Jesse. Both he and Damien were gone!

Mandy I will find a way back to you, I promise. I don't know what's going on but please take Cassie and get both of you back to the ranch. We will find our back somehow, some day. I love you.

"NOOOOO! JESSE!" I ran across the beach to the blanket where the guys had been sitting, they were both gone! I ran to the water; nothing. No one was around! I realized I was waist high in the water twisting in circles yelling for them. They couldn't have vanished into thin air! What happened, how could this be?! Where are they?

I got out of the water but couldn't walk, my legs felt like cottage cheese. I dropped to my knees hitting the sand sobbing. Jesse's face took all the space in my brain.

Six Months Later

"Mandy, I swear you'd be late to your own funeral! Your next class starts in twenty minutes!" Becca yelled from the edge of the Dressage arena. I could hear the aggravation in her voice. Becca is my right hand lady, I would be lost without her. She is so much more than my secretary. Becca is also my friend, colleague and kind of a second mom even though she's only 9 years older than me. She keeps me in line, that's a full-time job in itself.

"Okay, I'm on my way after this one jump, only one jump I promise." Becca rolled her eyes and headed back to the barn office. I turned my 16 hand sorrel Thoroughbred toward the one jump we had had problems with a few minutes ago. Zamira was an excellent jumper and had been very faithful to me all these years, my buddy.

I looked between his twitching ears and studied the upcoming jump. How many strides would he have to take, would he position himself correctly and take the jump on time or would he leap too soon? Those questions and more went through my head every time on an approach.

"Okay Zamira, one more time then you can retire for the day." I tightened the reins in my fingers and Zamira began to side-step slightly with anticipation as he sensed the moment. I barely squeezed my calves and he moved smoothly from a stand-still to a canter then I moved my upper body forward, closer to his head and finished getting my hands in position.

"You can do this baby."

The jump leered five strides ahead of us and I could feel the confidence in my steed as his ears wavered back and forth, his body felt like steel. I hugged my body closer into his neck and we felt like one. I moved my hands down closer toward his mouth. The front half of his body slowly rose to the height of the 4 foot jump and we both glided over the top. I peeked down for a split second and witnessed the jump and ground integrating into one scene. Zamira's front hooves hit the ground with a subtle thump while his back half and hooves slid gracefully behind us. Success! I rubbed his neck firmly and hugged as much of it as I could get my arms around.

"Good job, boy! You'll be a Grand Prix jumper in no time! How about those treats I promised you?" I let him prance around and side-step around the arena one last time then headed him to the gate. The cars of my students started pulling into the long drive that led to the barn.

"There's my cue boy. My class will be starting and Becca will have my head on a platter if I'm late." I jumped off, which was no small task and handed him over to Tony, my barn manager.

"Would you cool him off but leave the treats to me okay?"

"No problem." Tony grabbed the reins and headed back to the barn. I started up the small hill toward the barn to greet the kids when….

"Mandy, can you hear me? Mandy, it's Jesse."

"What the...?! Jesse?!" I wheeled around looking at the arena then the barn, toward the house, nothing. I knelt down on the grass sobbing. My mind went black.